Dating Cupid

Eve Langlais

Copyright © February 2011, Eve Langlais,
Copyright © 2nd Edition April 2016
Cover art by © Razzle Dazzle Design February
2011

Edited by Devin Govaere
Produced in Canada

Published by Eve Langlais
1606 Main Street, PO Box 151
Stittsville, Ontario, Canada, K2S1A3
http://www.EveLanglais.com

ISBN-13: 978-1530512140
ISBN-10: 153051214X

Prologue

The feminine moaning proved quite distinct from the moment Roxanne opened the door to the condo, a space she shared with her boyfriend, Kyle. *Maybe he's watching a dirty movie.*

Her head fuzzy from a cold, she clutched her paper bag from the pharmacy to her chest as she slid lazy feet along the hallway to the bedroom. She didn't do on purpose to move silently. She just couldn't be heard over the pants and groans she followed to the bedroom. Common sense tried to hammer through her denial but hit a brick wall in the form of the cold medicine she'd imbibed. Her cloudy mind and general malaise were the reason she'd come home early on a Tuesday afternoon in the first place.

Roxanne reached the bedroom, the door gaping open as usual, and peered in. She didn't recognize the blonde bouncing up and down on her boyfriend's groin, not that it mattered, although she did note how petite the yodeling cowgirl was— *the bitch.* And following on the heels of that thought was, *dirty cheating bastard.*

White-hot rage filled her at the incontrovertible evidence of Kyle's devious nature. With a fake, plastered smile and her body stiff with fury, she walked in shaking her paper bag from the pharmacy.

"Honey, I got that ointment you asked me to buy for that nasty rash under your balls."

Roxanne smirked as the blonde, with a look of shock, dove off Roxanne's soon-to-be ex-boyfriend. He, at least, had the grace to look sheepish as his afternoon romp dashed for the bathroom with a shouted, "You prick! You told me you were clean."

Kyle sat up in bed, his tousled hair and placating smile making Roxanne even angrier. *Tell me I'm imagining things now, you jerk.*

"It's not what it seems—" he started to say.

Roxanne scoffed. "Let me guess. You don't know how the hell she ended up naked and sitting on your cock?"

He had the decency to at least blush. "No, but I don't love her. It was just sex. You're the one I want to spend my life with."

Yeah, me and my money. "Get out." Roxanne crossed her arms and glared at him.

"What? Come on, can't we talk about this? You can't just mean to flush the last six months away because of one little mistake."

Roxanne's jaw dropped. "Little mistake? You were fucking another woman in our bed, and this after screwing me last night. So don't even try to claim it's because you were horny. There is only one mistake here, and it's mine for not seeing you sooner for the cheating prick you really are. Now, get out."

He stood with an indignant look, his

shriveled cock a tempting target for her foot. "You can't just throw me out. Where am I supposed to go?"

"I don't know, and I don't care. The condo is mine, as is everything in this place except for your clothes and DVDs. You have one hour to clear out before I show you that you chose the wrong woman to fuck around on."

Roxanne turned on her heel and walked away, smirking to herself as she heard the blonde castigate Kyle in shrill tones for giving her a venereal rash. Petty, but she still enjoyed it.

On her way out the door, she spied the mail on her side table. One envelope in particular caught her eye with its pink color. She snagged the pile as she walked out.

Before leaving for the gym and a frustration-melting workout, she hit the concierge's office and left strict orders about having Kyle escorted from the building with no option to return. She paid a high monthly fee for her condo security, and she intended to make good use of it.

I never want to see his smug face again.

Her rage carried her but only until she reached the privacy of her car in the underground garage. Once there, away from prying eyes, she finally lost control of her emotions, the tears falling like a hot rain shower. Alone, she shook and hugged herself, the betrayal of her supposed lover hurting her more deeply than she would ever admit to anyone.

Why does this keep happening to me? Don't I

deserve to find love?

She'd leaned over to grab a tissue from her glove box when she noticed, once again, the pink envelope peeking from the rest of her mail on the passenger seat.

She knew who it was from—Cupid's Dating Service. Abbreviated CDS, she'd signed on with them over a year ago, and unlike everyone else she knew who ranted about their successful matches, she'd yet to meet *the one*. Just look at their latest attempt—Kyle. Supposedly a perfect match for her, and yet, he'd turned out to be a cheating bastard. CDS was also the same idiotic company who'd set her up with her previous failed relationship with Roger who, it turned out, didn't like women and dated them only to please his mother. The same Fortune 500 Corporation that had sent her on several dates with Anthony, whose idea of bedroom fun included implements that belonged in a torture chamber.

Like a glutton for punishment, though, she kept going back to the dating service at the urging of her mother and friends, who swore the service was flawless in its choices.

Ha! I beg to differ. Whoever is in charge should be strung up by his balls because steering me wrong once, I can handle, two, I might excuse them by thinking they're still tweaking my perfect match, but the third one should have been Prince Charming himself. Instead, I got his alter ego, Prince Cheating.

She tore open the pink envelope to find a card. On the front it read in big letters

"*Congratulations*" followed by smaller print inside that said, "*We at Cupid's Dating Service would like to congratulate you on reaching the six month mark with your true love. May your love today still be as strong when you hit your twenty-year anniversary.*"

Roxanne laughed. And laughed. She laughed so hard the tears rolled even thicker down her face. It took a while for her hysterical mirth to die down, but when it did, with hiccupping sobs, a plan formed in her mind, one to make sure that corporate Cupid with its money-grabbing scheme stopped screwing lonely woman like herself.

One hundred percent guarantee love match, my ass. I'm going to show the world what a fraud these guys really are. Screw Cupid.

Chapter One

"What do you mean we've shown no growth again?" questioned Maverick, owner and CEO of Cupid's Dating Service. He'd also coined their catch phrase, "*One shot for love.*" He directed his query to the head of accounting with whom he was teleconferenced in with, along with the marketing department head.

"There's no denying it. Something is causing people to not sign up, and even worse, we've seen a few new signups drop out of our service before we've even had a chance to send them on a date."

Maverick paced the plush carpet in his high-rise office, baffled at his spiraling loss of business, a first since he'd started the company almost five years before. "That makes no sense."

"Um, I think I can explain," interjected Jane from marketing. "I think that our loss of popularity has to do with a disgruntled client."

Maverick's brows shot up. "So their first match didn't work out. It happens occasionally. Set the unhappy client up for free with the right one."

"Actually, she's been set up with three matches, all of them free of charge at this point, but none have worked out according to her."

Maverick stopped his circle walking and

turned to face the phone. "Three failed suitors? Impossible," he said in an incredulous tone. "I programmed the system myself. It's almost foolproof." It had taken him years, but the finished product had more than exceeded his expectations and, in return, that of his clients. His success rate until now was a whopping 100 percent with most people being set up with their true love on the first date. Two at the most. Three was absolutely unheard of.

"We've been over the complainant's file numerous times," Jane said in reply. "We even rechecked her parameters. The computer actually spit out a list of names as possible matches."

"A list?" Maverick found himself even more baffled. While a person could have more than one true love match, more than a handful was impossible. The parameters involved in a successful relationship were many and varied.

"We've never seen anything like it. She actually had dozens of names proposed by the system. We honed it down and set her up on the basis of the most likely to appeal. All of them, according to the computer, should have been perfect matches."

"And?" Maverick queried. He sat in his office chair and drummed his fingers on his desk in agitation.

"We were *really* wrong in each case."

Maverick didn't ask her the details. Jane was thorough when she performed research. If she said they'd fucked up, then he believed her, even if it galled him to admit his computer program could have flaws. "So input everything again and find her the right one this time. We must have messed something up the first time."

"That's just it. We've re-entered her information numerous times. Each time, it's the same thing. Even weirder, each time we run her profile, the computer spits out a different list of men."

Dammit, the system has a bug. So much for relaxing this weekend. It looked as if he'd spend it tracking down the error in his program. "Send me up her file, and I'll find her a match the old-fashioned way."

"Um, well, that's just it. She's made it blatantly clear she doesn't want our help any longer, even though we've offered it to her completely free of charge at this point."

Maverick frowned. "Fine, let's put the issue of her failed dates to the side for a moment. Explain, please, exactly how one disgruntled client is affecting our bottom line."

"She's embarked on a media campaign to discredit us."

"What?" Maverick shouted. He reined in his temper and rubbed his temple, trying to ease the building headache. "Sorry for yelling. Please continue."

Jane hesitantly filled him in. "She's got a Facebook fan page denouncing our service and is calling for other dissatisfied clients to join her. She's also got a blog where she's written some pretty vehement stuff. And her latest campaign is to run ads alongside ours asking people to boycott the big corporations looking to steal their money for the promise of a false happily ever after. They're actually quite catchy ads. I'm surprised you haven't seen them what with the huge 'Screw Cupid' logo she's created and plastered in several major media outlets."

"I'll sue her ass," Maverick swore. He wouldn't allow one irate female—some shrewish spinster who probably wouldn't know love if it smacked her in the face—to destroy his empire. He'd worked too hard to streamline his dating service, which, in turn, freed up his time, to have one irrational female ruin it.

"The legal department says it would be better to send a cease and desist notice first and, if she then refuses to halt her smear campaign, have a sit-down with her to see if it can be resolved out of court. They claim suing her will put us in an even worse light with the public."

"Fine. First, we try and get her to stop. If she refuses, then we'll pull out the big guns."

Jane hesitantly said, "But wouldn't it just be better to find her love? We could do it the old-fashioned way, in her case. Then, if we could get her to recant, I bet it would drive business to us instead."

"I'll think about it," Maverick said, even as he knew he had no intention of rewarding the harridan intent on destroying his empire. Having already been screwed over by a woman in his past, he'd promised himself to never allow it again. "In the meantime, though, we are not going to take this sitting down. Get the legal department to send a letter demanding she halt her actions. And don't make it too nice. I am serious about wanting her to stop."

"Yes, sir."

Maverick thumbed the speakerphone off and sighed. *I try to make everybody happy, and as usual, there always has to be one person who just refuses.* Even more troubling, though, was the fact that his dating program, developed over years of hard work, had failed in the first place. *What went wrong?* He'd designed everything himself and imbued it with magic, his magic. Maverick didn't just play at being Cupid. He was the one and only Cupid.

And, dammit, I won't go back to the old ways. Shooting someone with an arrow? How archaic. Not to mention time consuming. *Also, by finding them true love instead of forcing it on them at the tip of my arrow means even more happiness for the lucky couples.*

In these modern times, love, especially given the population explosion and his lack of staff, needed help. His dating service, conceived many years ago, had seemed the perfect cover to do his job as god of love without all the hassle.

Perfect, that was, until now.

The glitch made him wonder if he should halt the expansion plans to hit the Canadian and European market. Currently, he had his lackeys running around with almost no respite in those areas, targeting people with love arrows and hoping they didn't accidentally fall in love with the wrong person.

No, he couldn't allow one shrew to halt progress—and a much-needed break. He'd go forth into those markets bringing true love to those who wished it. As for the woman who kept spitting in love's eye—and hence, his—maybe he'd send one of his minions to give it to her the old-fashioned way. Just thinking about shooting the faceless woman in the ass with a love arrow made him laugh.

And if I'm lucky, she'll fall in love with the opposite of what she is attracted to.

Chapter Two

For a second time Roxanne read the registered letter, and her ire increased with each pompous line.

"...cease the slandering of Cupid's Dating Service. Refusal to comply will result in legal action..."

She balled the missive up and, with a windup pitch, threw it into her blue recycling bin. *If you don't like my campaign, then try and stop me. You aren't the only one with legal ties. That and I've got luck on my side—well, except when it comes to men.*

Inspiration struck, and she retrieved the crumpled-up letter from the bin. She placed it in her scanner, and minutes later, she'd added the letter to her campaign to discredit CDS. She grinned as she imagined their reaction.

Although a month had passed since she'd caught Kyle cheating and thrown him out, her emotions still ached, their bruising at his, and other hands, not an easy thing to heal from.

Is it too much to ask that I find the one? A part of her realized that not all the blame lay with CDS. Heck, before she'd even signed on with them, her love life—make that lack of—had been a sore point. A magnet for losers, Roxanne had dated more than her fair share of men, and without fail, each and every one had screwed her over. CDS and its failures after its guarantees and glowing recommendations from friends had just been the sloppy icing on top of a collapsing cake of hope. *I've had it. Screw men and screw love.*

She'd found solace in her work to bring the corporate dating giant down. Although it surprised her it had taken them this long to finally respond to her smear campaign.

Roxanne received the expected answer to her actions a few days later, but not in the form she'd expected. The familiar pink envelope was hand delivered by a bike courier to her office downtown. Tucked inside, she found a handwritten missive from the CEO himself. Intrigued he'd actually taken the time to write her—*it took him long enough*—she read the letter with interest. In a nutshell, she received an apology for her displeasure with their service, and the letter writer asked if she would agree to a sit-down meeting with the owner of the company, Maverick Eros himself. Roxanne smirked. Of all the names in the world, surely his was one of the cheesiest—*I highly doubt it's the name he was born with.*

Her first impulse was to shrug off his latest attempt to placate her, but she couldn't deny a curiosity to meet the man behind the whole scam. Put a face to the jerk who had caused her such heartache by promising a forever-after love. *Punch the man who raised my hopes and dashed them.*

Roxanne dressed somberly for the meeting in a black skirt and a black silk blouse topped with a short-waisted white jacket for a contrasting color. Armed for battle, she went to meet her nemesis without calling first, preferring to catch him off guard.

The CDS corporation headquarters were situated just outside the downtown core. She drove her car to her ambush meeting pondering what she'd say to Mr. Eros if he had the guts to face her. In order to arm herself with knowledge, she'd queried him online, and while his name cropped up often in the romantic circles, the man himself was an enigma. She couldn't find a photo of him anywhere, although she did discover he was in his late thirties and single. *Ha, just more proof his dating business is a scam. How good can the service be if its owner can't even find love?*

She found the CDS building. It was hard to miss with its arrowlike shape, which loomed impressively over her. *I wonder how many broken hearts it's built on?*

Roxanne walked through the main doors, her heels clacking loudly on the gleaming marble floors. The vestibule echoed emptily, bare of people except for a receptionist situated in the middle of the vast space behind a circular desk. The blonde lifted her head, which was adorned with a headset. With a perky smile, the receptionist said, "Welcome to Cupid's Dating Service. How may we help you today?"

"I'm here to see the owner."

The bubbly blonde's smile didn't falter. "No problem, ma'am. Do you have a meeting scheduled?"

Roxanne girded herself to argue. "More or less. He sent me a letter asking to meet. So, here I am."

The receptionist's smile turned into a frown. "I'm sorry, ma'am, but without an appointment, I'm afraid I can't let you up. While Mr. Eros loves to meet new people, he is quite busy. But I'm sure if you call his secretary, she could schedule something."

"Listen here"—Roxanne craned over the desk's counter to peek at her nametag—"Lisa. If I walk out this door, then your boss can forget about me dropping the Screw Cupid campaign. He's the one who thought we should speak, not me. So, either you get me up to see him right this minute, or I walk out and he can talk to my lawyers."

Lisa's mouth rounded in an *O* of surprise, but not for the reason Roxanne expected. "You're *her*. Why didn't you say so?"

"Her who?" Roxanne queried, confused at Lisa's reaction.

"We've all been talking about you. Everyone is quite abuzz. You're the only unsatisfied customer we've ever had."

The "Really?" emerged in an incredulous drawl. "I find it hard to believe I'm the first person to ever complain about your service."

"Oh, every now and then it takes a second try to get a true love match right. Mr. Eros says sometimes it's necessary to date the wrong person first in order to appreciate the perfect person when they do come along. But it's unheard of for the system to strike out three times."

The girl became the recipient of a frown, mostly because Roxanne didn't believe her. As solid company employees went, this Lisa was taking loyalty a little too far. No matchmaking service was that good. Although, if their claim was true, then it would certainly explain the lack of other clients coming forth to join her in complaining. The only support she'd garnered was from people who'd thought of using the service but then abstained after hearing her story. However, Roxanne knew there had to be other unsatisfied clients out there. *Because I refuse to believe I'm the only person ever not able to find love.*

Time to try a different tactic. "Have you, or anyone you know, tried the service?"

Lisa beamed. "I tried it and couldn't be happier. It's how I met my husband, Ralph. It was love at first sight," she sighed. "My sister and cousin, too, have also used it. Now they're both engaged. Mom's next." Lisa looked at Roxanne with a wrinkled nose. "I still can't believe it didn't work for you. I mean it's not even like you're ugly. The boys down in the mailroom had a bet going that you were a hag."

Roxanne wanted to blast the girl, but to her annoyance, her cute and perky attitude made it hard to hold on to her anger. *A hag though?* An understandable theory, she guessed, given that, unlike other dating services, CDS didn't use profile images at all. The matches were based on a person's attributes instead of exterior appearance. *I wonder how many people turned around and walked away after getting set up with someone who didn't appeal at all. And why haven't they come forward to join me in complaining?* Her ire returned as she wondered just what the hell was wrong with her that she couldn't find love like everyone else. "Now that we've clarified who I am, can I go meet your boss now?"

Lisa smiled. "Oh, of course you can. Take the elevator on the back wall all the way up. I'll call his secretary and let her know you're coming."

Roxanne walked to the row of elevators in bemusement. She hadn't actually imagined they'd let her in. She'd actually looked forward to getting kicked out so she could post on her blog and Facebook page that the faceless corporation didn't care about the little customer in its greed to collect their dues. Finding out that her case was the topic of discussion was shocking to say the least, as was the news she was alone in her complaint.

The plush elevator climbed smoothly to the thirteenth floor. An odd number, given many larger buildings tended to skip the thirteenth altogether over foolish superstition.

The electric door slid open onto a spacious waiting area dominated by a large desk manned by a petite, gray-haired woman. Roxanne strode up to the desk expecting to have to restate her case, but the secretary jumped up and smiled in welcome.

"Goodness, you aren't at all what we expected. Aren't you just lovely? And tall. Lucky you."

Roxanne reeled from the woman's enthusiastic demeanor. Somehow, she'd expected the money-grubbing owner to have a battle-axe as a secretary. "Thank you. So, am I to meet with your boss, or should I just be on my way?" She wished the woman would throw her out and give her some justification to complain about their treatment of her, but so far, nothing was turning out the way she'd expected.

"Oh, of course you can see him. Mr. Eros will be so glad you've come. We're all awfully sorry your experience with us has been so poor. But I'm sure Mr. Eros will take care of all that. The man is like a god when it comes to love." The gray-haired matron tittered as she led the way to a pair of impressive wooden doors. She swung them open and announced, "Miss Roxanne Fortuna to see you, sir."

"Thank you, Mrs. Pettibone. If you could see we're not disturbed," replied a low-timbered voice that sent shivers dancing up Roxanne's spine.

"Of course, sir." Mrs. Pettibone stepped out of the way and motioned at Roxanne to enter. "Good luck," the matron whispered with a wink.

Taking a deep breath that did nothing to slow down her galloping heart, Roxanne entered the lair of the CEO.

And was almost struck dumb. *Dear heavens, the man is gorgeous.*

Taller than her five-foot-nine inches, he towered over her, even though she wore heels. A well-cut suit hugged his broad shoulders, and the blue of it brought out the brightness of his eyes. His blonde hair, cut short, hugged his head with tight curls. He looked like a Greek statue come to life with a face of chiseled perfection, lips curved into a perfect sensual bow and a smile to melt her insides—and dampen her undies.

Roxanne blinked and tried to shake off the strange urge she had to throw herself at him and kiss his gently smiling lips.

He's the definition of corporate evil, no matter how good-looking. Come on, Roxanne, no getting distracted. Her inner pep talk made her feet move across the plush carpeting to meet him as he rounded his desk, his eyes never once leaving hers. She blamed her erratic heartbeat on nerves.

He thrust his hand out and said, in a voice that made her tingle all too pleasantly, "Hello, Ms. Fortuna. I am so glad you could make the time to see me. My name is Maverick Eros."

Then his fingers clasped hers, and she just about swooned at the electricity that sizzled at the touch and the awareness that slammed the rest of her.

What the heck is happening?

Chapter Three

When his secretary buzzed him to announce his one and only ever disgruntled client had come calling, Maverick had braced himself for a lot of things, including the fact that whoever he'd face would probably have an ugly exterior to match her attitude.

Instead, breathtaking perfection walked into his office.

Perhaps not beautiful by modern-day definitions, but most certainly by his. Her model height—a perfect match for his—was enhanced with heels. But whereas today's models were bone racks, this beauty was lush in all the right places. From her juicy lips to her tightly harnessed bosom to the indent of her waist, which flared out into womanly hips, she reminded him of the Rubenesque beauties of old. An old-style, plush frame where a man could lose himself in softness and never want to leave. In other words, the type he preferred.

Stunned, he said and did nothing, even as he knew his lack of reaction must appear odd. She broke the spell, and at her approach, he circled his desk and extended his hand.

And lightning struck.

A sense of rightness hit him with the weight of a freight train and sucked the air from his lungs. He was glad to see her eyes open wide, the effect apparently not one-sided.

Maverick pulled his hand away with reluctance, peeking quickly at his unblemished skin. He saw no sign she'd pricked him, not that he expected one given his reaction before he'd even touched her. But he'd certainly check himself thoroughly later for any signs of another *accident*.

I won't go through hell again like I did last time I accidentally poked myself with my own curse of love.

As Cupid, descended from Venus and Mars, also known as Aphrodite and Ares, he'd bestowed the gift—in his mind, curse—of love for thousands of years. Only once before had he fallen victim to his own brand of magic, something that he'd paid dearly for and had no intention of ever repeating.

Love is for mortals. Me, I'll take peace and quiet, thank you very much.

Realizing he was wool gathering again as Ms. Fortuna eyed him with a blush, he waved at her to take a seat in one of the comfortable armchairs he had set in front of his floor-to-ceiling windows. The view was magnificent and caught her eye as she sat down. Unfortunately, he'd seen it thousands of time before, so instead, he found himself captured by the sight of her skirt pulling up over her stocking-covered thighs, plump thighs that he could so easily imagine himself between.

Jumping up from his seat with a semi hard-on, he called over his shoulder. "Would you like some coffee?" Whether she said yes or not, he needed something to occupy his hands and thoughts. *Where is my legendary control?* Apparently gone to his cock, which, roused by the sight of the luscious Ms. Fortuna, refused to lie down and play dead.

"Yes, a coffee would be nice, thank you. Black, please."

Somehow, he'd known she wouldn't take it with cream or sugar. Straightforward and rich to the taste, just like her. Maverick wanted to bang his head on the wall. He needed to stop thinking of her in terms of sex. *I've got to get her out of here and visit my mother. Maybe she can get this spell off of me.* He didn't believe for one minute his intense attraction was natural. Not when he'd sworn off women, especially human ones.

Maverick carried the brimming mugs back, almost scalding himself when the fleeting touch of her fingers jolted him. He heard her intake of breath and knew she'd experienced it, too. She grabbed the mug, her light touch brushing him again and shooting his iron control to hell and back.

Maverick sat down hard and forced himself to look out the window, even as her magnetic presence kept attempting to pull his gaze back to her. But it was as if Fate—his mother's friend— herself was against him, for he could see Ms. Fortuna's reflection in the glass. He couldn't look away as she flicked her tongue out from between her luscious lips to test the brew. He found himself riveted when her throat moved as she swallowed a mouthful—he could so easily picture her swallowing something else. And he almost groaned aloud when she smoothed her skirt down, her hand brushing her sheer black nylons. *Is she teasing me on purpose?*

"Tell me what you want." Spoken perhaps a more tab brusque than necessary. Her fault because he couldn't help but think, *Say me and I will strip you naked right here and now to lick every inch of your body.*

To his relief—and his cock's disappointment—she replied, "I think your dating service is a sham."

Her blunt accusation forced him to face her, and his indignation at her words allowed him to regain some semblance of control. "I hardly think that one complaint is enough on which to base that theory."

"Who says it's one complaint?" she retorted.

He leaned back, the pending argument toning down his desire as he defended his life's work. "Fine, I'll bite." *Any part of your body that you want.* "Where's your list of complainants?"

Her cheeks flushed, and Maverick crossed his legs as his shaft perked up in interest again—of course it could have had to do with the fleeting image he'd had of her with the same flushed cheeks, but on her back, naked, as he pounded into her soft flesh.

The erotic image was rapidly forgotten with her next words. "I don't have a list. But I'm sure it's just a matter of time. After all, I can't be the only one whose love life you've screwed up."

He heard the hurt under her terse words, and he wanted to drop to his knees and swear he'd never allow anyone to hurt her again. *Hot damn, whatever spell I'm under is potent.* He forced himself to focus back on the conversation at hand. "If you want reimbursement, then consider it done."

Her eyes sparked. "This isn't about money. I've already had everything credited back to me. This is about false promises to consumers. Your company promises true love. All I got, though, was shafted."

And your heart broken, a feeling I understand all too well. Having gone through the pain of betrayal, he could grudgingly concede that she had a right to her anger. However, understanding didn't mean he could allow her to continue in her vendetta. "I'm sorry if the men we set you up with hurt you. Let us make it up to you. Give us another chance to find your one." But Maverick almost growled at the thought of her dating—touching—another man.

"I've given you three chances. You failed."

"Yes, your file shows we set you up with three perfect matches, but it doesn't say what happened. The last one lasted six months according to our records. I don't suppose you'd care to elaborate?"

Her color heightened as her eyes flashed with ire. "Why? So you can mock me?"

He let his eyes meet hers and couldn't look away. "I would never make fun of someone's pain. I know all too well love can hurt." He had the emotional scars to prove it. "Please believe me when I say it was never my intention that you be falsely led. If there's a problem with our programming, then I want to correct it. Perhaps your tale will help me find the glitch."

Instead of replying, she stood abruptly. He shot to his feet in time to grab the half-filled mug that she thrust at him.

"Forget it. I'm overreacting. It's my own fault for expecting a company to give me something I can't find on my own. I'll drop the campaign. Sorry to have bothered you."

Maverick wanted to retort—and beg her to stay—but she walked away from him. Her rounded behind swayed as she left, drying his mouth and sticking his tongue to the roof of his mouth. By the time he realized she was serious—and after he'd pictured that lush ass naked and bent over for him—she'd disappeared.

He knew he should count himself lucky. She'd agreed to stop badmouthing his company. But all he could think of was, when would he see her again?

Maverick shook his head, but he couldn't dislodge her from his mind. Her scent, her look, his desire to hold her, hug and …

That's it. Time to visit my mother and find out who's cursed me with my own brand of magic.

Chapter Four

Roxanne made it home in a blur, thanking her auto-pilot reflexes that allowed her to drive in a state of stunned disbelief.

From the moment she'd met the impossibly handsome Maverick Eros, she'd pictured him—naked—in various situations that made her hotter than the desert on a sunny day. All her mentally practiced arguments and logic disappeared in his presence. When she'd caught him crossing his legs to hide an obvious erection—*he found me attractive*—she'd wanted to jump him and taste his delicious-looking mouth.

His sincerity in regards to her situation had torn down all the arguments she'd used to armor herself. He'd even courteously apologized and asked for her help. And the fleeting pain she'd glimpsed in his eyes had made him only more attractive. *He understands what I'm going through.* When he'd spoken of finding her true match, she'd wanted to cry, "He's sitting right in front of me." At that moment, she'd realized she needed to escape.

She found herself baffled by her out-of-proportion attraction to him. She'd never reacted so lustily to a stranger before, and she'd met her share of handsome fellows. Not to mention, any other man who'd had such an obvious sexual interest in her would have found himself treated to the sharp edge of her tongue. Instead of lambasting him, though, she'd fled his office like a blushing schoolgirl, promising to halt her harassment.

Unfortunately for her, she happened to be a woman of her word. She found the task of taking down the websites and blogs devoted to the crumbling of his empire helped to somewhat guide her thoughts in directions other than what he hid under his suit.

However, stopping her campaign didn't take long. She'd no sooner finished than her hands began to idly rub the skin of her thighs, picturing his big, capable ones doing the stroking instead.

Roxanne cursed aloud. "Stupid, annoying man! I think he cast a spell on me." The jerk must have laced her coffee with some kind of magical potion, probably bought off the fairy black market. Much as it was frowned upon, the pesky winged critters persisted in selling taboo magic to humans.

And no it wasn't strange for her to believe in magic and fey creatures, she was after all a demigod, not that she enjoyed the reminder. She'd left the godly realm for the mortal one as a teen when she got tired of the games played among the deities.

Even though she'd left, she did retain some connections. It just so happened she knew a person to call for help with a possible love spell.

"Mom," she called aloud, knowing her

meddling mother would hear her.

A swirl of colored air appeared in front of her and coalesced into the smiling form of her mother. "Roxi, darling. Whatever is the matter? Did you change your mind about me killing that disgusting Kyle?"

Roxanne frowned. "Mom, I told you. No using your godly powers on me or anyone involved with me." Although she couldn't help hoping Kyle would suffer a bit of bad luck, her mother's godly specialty. Roxanne wasn't just a superbly skilled stockbroker who'd built herself a fortune in only three years. She was the daughter of the one and only Annonaria Fortuna, also known as Lady Luck and the goddess of fortune, whether it be good or not.

"I still don't understand this desire of yours to live like a mortal. You're a demigod, for Zeus's sake, Roxi. Why do you torture yourself with this human mode of living?" Her mother made a moue of distaste as she ran her finger over the mantel of Roxanne's cold, stone fireplace and held up the dusty result.

"Because I like it," grumbled Roxanne, flopping on the couch as her mother brought up the bone of contention between them. Roxanne wanted to live a normal life without the influence of her mother and other gods. She'd seen firsthand growing up the havoc that could, and would, happen to gods, even demi ones. It was the reason she'd lost her father. A mere mortal, in love with Lady Luck, he'd ended up the target of another god pissed at her mom for his string of bad luck in the casinos.

Roxanne had sworn a vow as she cried over her father's grave that she would stay away from the machinations of the supernatural crowd to live a normal life. So far, she'd done fairly well. She had a great job, a fabulous apartment, and fantastic friends. The one black spot, though, was her lack of a man, make that a lover, in her life.

Her mother sat down beside her and hugged her close. "My poor baby. I can tell by your face you're upset. Tell me what's wrong."

"I'm horny." Roxanne blushed as soon as the words—even if honest—popped out of her mouth.

Lady Luck laughed. "That's not a problem. Actually, I'm happy to hear you're over that disgusting slimeball, Kyle. Who's the lucky man?"

"Maverick Eros, but you're misunderstanding. I think someone cast some kind of lust spell on me because, from the moment I met the man, I just wanted to jump him."

"Are you talking about Venus's son? Oh, have you two finally met? How wonderful. Isn't he the most charming and handsome man you've ever encountered?" her mother gushed.

Roxanne sat up straight. "Venus's son? You mean the real Cupid? He's the owner of CDS?"

"Well, of course he is, darling. And doing a fine job of it, too, from what I hear." Then her mother, as if remembering Roxanne's dating difficulties, amended her statement with, "Most of the time anyways. You know, I'm sure those first three bozos were just an accident. It's probably your demigod status messing his methods up. Have you told him you're my daughter?"

"Of course not. Heck, I didn't even know he was a god." But knowing who he was perhaps explained some of her attraction to him. As god of love, he probably exuded some kind of manwhore vibe.

"God or not, he's a very nice boy. I tried to help him during his divorce from that nasty human who tricked him, but she engaged her own celestial help, countering my efforts," her mother said with a scowl.

"The god in charge of love is divorced?" Roxanne snorted. "Gee, now there's a reason to let him decide my love life. No thank you."

"You really should give him a chance. He's really decent when you get to know him."

Roxanne's eyes widened in horror at her mom's hint. "I am not dating a god, especially not some sexual deviant who probably beds a different woman every night."

"But—"

Roxanne glared at her mother. "No. Now, chances are I won't ever run into him again, but in case I do, how do I fight his sexual magnetism?"

"What do you mean?"

"I mean how do I fight his cupidness? You know, his ability to make women horny for him?"

Her mother howled with laughter. "Oh, darling, he doesn't have that power. Sounds to me like you're just plain old attracted to him."

"Impossible," Roxanne grumbled. "He's not even my type. You know I like dark-haired men, not blue-eyed blonds who are prettier than I am. Check me for spells. It's the only thing that makes sense."

Her mother sighed and rolled her eyes as she stood and inspected Roxanne for spells. A few minutes later, she shook her head with a smile. "I don't see any spells."

At those words, Roxanne groaned aloud. "Un-freaking-real. Attracted to some womanizer. Well, at least I don't have to worry about accidentally meeting him again. I'm done with CDS."

"If you say so, darling. Now, are we still on for dinner on Saturday?" her mother asked, changing the subject.

Roxanne held in a sigh. *Great, another dinner with my mother and her newest boyfriend, some Norse demigod who's young enough to be my brother.* Much as she wanted to bail, she didn't want to hurt her mother's feelings. "Yes, I'm still coming. I'll bring the wine."

"Perfect," her mother replied, clapping her hands. "See you then. Oh, and try to dress up a bit. I've invited a few friends to join us."

Before Roxanne could protest she wasn't in the mood to hang out with a bunch of gods lamenting the good old days where humans worshipped them and they raced chariots in the sky, her mother popped out of sight.

Roxanne sighed and sat back down. *No spell. That sucks, especially since now I have no idea how to get the picture of Cupid out of my mind and, even worse, the urge I have to see him again.*

Why couldn't he have been a fat cherub in diapers?

Chapter Five

Maverick strode across the polished marble floors of his mother's palace in Olympus and bellowed for her. "Mother!"

A giggle preceded his mother appearing from a side chamber. Venus straightened her diaphanous robes as she strode toward Maverick with a welcoming smile. "Cupie, baby. What brings you here?"

Maverick fought a wince at his hated nickname. No matter how much he begged, his mother persisted in using the childish term of endearment. He embraced his mother, noting the distinct smell of his father's aftershave clinging to her. "Where's Dad?"

"Right here, son," said his father, emerging from the same side chamber, his face flushed, also straightening his robes.

Maverick groaned. "Again? Don't you guys ever stop?"

"Never," his parents exclaimed with wide grins.

Maverick shook his head, even as his parents' affection for each other humbled him. Theirs was a true love match not induced with arrows in the ass or spells. Just an old-fashioned affection for each other, along with a heavy dose of lust. *As god of love, you'd think I could easily find the same for myself.*

"What brings you home? I wasn't expecting you until Saturday for dinner," his mother asked.

Maverick paced the polished marble floors, as his dilemma in the form of one shapely client rose with ease in his mind's eye. "I think someone's put me under some kind of spell. I need you to take it off."

Immediately, his father's eyes flashed. "The nerve. I'll teach them to mess with my son." As god of war, his father could definitely make a spell caster's life miserable, not to mention painful.

His mother, her face creased in concern, asked, "What kind of spell, baby?" She forced him to stop his pacing to run her hands up and down the length of his body, her magic tickling his skin as it searched for the source of his discontent.

"Some kind of lust or love spell," he replied with disgust. Not a very hearty disgust, for in the grips of infatuation with the lovely Ms. Fortuna, he found it hard to muster a lot of dislike for what was actually a pleasurable—if unwelcome—feeling.

His mother tittered, and his father guffawed as he said, "Did some harpy get her claws in you, son?"

"Is she a goddess? How's her lineage?" His mother, ever the practical matchmaker.

"She's just a normal human, so you can get that gleam out of your eye, Mother." Ever since his disastrous first and only marriage, five hundred years before, Venus had made it her mission to keep an eye open for new daughter-in-law prospects. Never mind the fact that Maverick never intended to get snared in the marriage trap again. His mother seemed determined to find him his one true love, whether he liked it or not.

"No need to sound so disparaging, son. There's many a fine human out there," his father said, only to recant when his mother slapped him in the arm. "Not as fine as your mother, of course, but not everyone can be as lucky as I."

"I know there are some great humans out there, but honestly, after the fiasco with Psyche, I am not interested in traveling that road again. So, your assistance, Mother, in removing the spell and, even better, at pointing out the culprit responsible, which would be appreciated." Then he could show them with his fist what he thought of their practical joke.

His mother frowned as she stepped back from him. "I hate to break it to you, Cupie, but there's no spell on you of any kind, not even the love-arrow variety."

"Impossible," Maverick replied, even as his heart panicked. "She's a human. Plus, she hates me."

"Perhaps you are mistaken in your feelings. You work too hard. Get some rest. Stay for a plate of homemade food. I've got your favorite— lasagna—in the oven."

"I guess since I'm here it wouldn't hurt to have a bite." Maverick let his mother lead him into the large kitchen and park him on a stool by the massive granite-topped island.

As his mother prepared a salad while keeping up a lively banter with his father, Maverick sipped on his wine and couldn't help his mind wandering back to Ms. Fortuna. *Roxanne.*

He could picture her so easily—and his cock twitched a hello in response. *Just because I'm attracted to her doesn't mean I'm in love. It's long past time I got some action. Perhaps built-up horniness is to blame for my reaction to her.*

A simple solution then. Find a woman—*Roxanne*—to assuage his arousal on. Unfortunately, only one name and face came to mind. Maverick groaned and lowered his head into his hands.

"Dinner's ready," his mother announced in a bright tone of voice.

He took his place at the table and tore into the steaming plate of lasagna, with extra cheese, of course, served with garlic bread. He interspersed the hot food with refreshing bites of his crisp Caesar salad. His mother might enjoy many names and roles as goddess, but when it came to cooking, he personally thought she rocked.

"So, Saturday, instead of having dinner here, we're going over to Lady's Luck's," his mother said, her words breaking into his happy eating zone.

Maverick stopped chewing and swallowed. "Then I'll see you the following week, I guess." He'd long ago stopped associating with the other gods. It made his life so much simpler that way.

His mother looked stricken. "Oh, don't cancel. You know how I love seeing you. And won't it be fun to see Lucky again? She used to dote on you so much when you were a baby."

Maverick groaned, but for an entirely different reason than a moment ago. "Aw, Mom. Please do not try and guilt me. Don't forget I was married to the best. I see right through you."

His mother sniffed. "Yes, I know I'm so baaad. No need to rub it in my face. I've tried to move past the misdeeds of my youth."

Maverick's father glared at him as he patted Venus's hand. "Now, now my little nymph. Don't cry. I'll thrash his unworthy hide and send him to the mines of Hell to work out some of his disrespectfulness." Venus gave Ares a tremulous smile in reply.

Maverick sighed and caved to the inevitable. "The two of you are impossible. Fine. You win. I'll go."

Venus immediately clapped her hands. "Fabulous. And wear something black. It brings out the blue of your eyes."

Maverick groaned again as his father chuckled. *Caught again by the queen of manipulation.* "Why do you guys always do that to me?"

"It never grows old. But next time, add a little more grovel. It makes your mother happy," his father said with a wink.

Maverick joined the laughter as, once again, his parents managed to distract him with their love for him and each other. A real love that he'd never actually experienced for or from anyone else, an affection given freely and without remorse.

My parents, the most perfect shining example of love. Make me gag.

Chapter Six

Roxanne whined, even though she knew she sounded childish. "Mom, do I have to stay? I am not in the mood to make nice with your friends."

"Oh stop your bellyaching and finish setting the table. Why, one of the guests used to be your absolute favorite adopted aunt when you were little."

"If she's so special, then why did I stop seeing her?" Roxanne asked, slapping down the silverware on the polished surface of the massive dark wood table in the dining room.

"Sometimes you get busy," her mother replied vaguely, tweaking the centerpiece of roses intertwined with ivy and candles.

Roxanne tried to think back to who she didn't see any more that used to be a regular visitor, but at almost three hundred years of age, she had a lot of damned memories. She'd met and gotten to know hosts of people—not all of them human, or sane—during her lifetime.

What bugged her more was the sense of anticipation, as if she knew something momentous prepared to occur. She didn't like or trust it at all. *It almost feels like someone's meddling with me and my future.*

"You're not matchmaking, are you?"

Roxanne asked, casting a suspicious glance at her mother.

"Who, me?" her mother asked with eyes a little too wide. The doorbell rang, and with a bright smile, her mother almost ran to answer it. *This is beginning to look more and more like a setup.* Roxanne sighed. *Hopefully, this time he'll only have two arms, unlike her last matchmaking attempt. Slapping down eight hands attempting to grope is not my idea of a fun evening.*

Her mother's newest boyfriend, an awfully good-looking demigod from the Norse side of the immortal kingdom, reached the front door first. With a bright white smile, he answered just as her mother skidded to a stop at his side. Roxanne turned away, the wide-open space still carrying to her the sounds of their voices.

Hellos were exchanged, along with the sound of air kisses. Then, a velvety, familiar voice spoke. Roxanne froze in the act of putting down a knife. *No, she wouldn't dare.*

Oh yes, she had. Roxanne turned with a frozen look of disbelief to the man in the doorway, handing her mother a bouquet of flowers. Her eyes darted from side to side, searching for an escape. But her mother had positioned her well. She couldn't flee without attracting attention—*his attention.* Her nipples tightened at the thought.

She whirled back to the table and tried to control her racing pulse and woken libido. She could do nothing, however, about the moisture dampening her cleft and panties. She blamed the erotic dreams she'd suffered nightly since their meeting, where he held the starring role—naked. *And now he's here in the flesh—his scrumptious, manly flesh.* Roxanne groaned. *No way am I staying now.*

The voices faded in volume, and she let out a breath as she realized they'd moved into the family room area across the way. Maybe if she sidled sideways with her back to them, she could escape to the kitchen and the door to outside and freedom.

Roxanne didn't even question her frantic desire to escape. Something about Maverick Eros called to her. Made her heart beat faster and her breath hitch. Gave her the wettest dreams. Awoke a longing in her.

She didn't trust it. *No one falls in love at first sight. Especially not with Cupid. Unless…*

A nasty thought occurred to her, and suddenly, she didn't care if she came face to face with him or not.

She whirled and almost ran into him, as her mother had snuck up with Maverick in tow.

His brilliant blue eyes went wide with shock when they beheld her. "*Roxanne.*" He whispered her name, and she almost melted into a puddle at his feet.

Her intense reaction brought back her anger and accusation. She flung it at him triumphantly. "Ha, I knew there was no way I could actually want you. You put a spell on me. A love spell with one of your arrows, didn't you? That's why I can't stop thinking of you."

Roxanne glared at Maverick Eros, the god

of love, and fought the urge to kiss the look of disbelief on his face.

She didn't fight her urge to slap him, though, when he laughed.

Chapter Seven

Maverick handed the bottle of wine over to Lady Luck, Lucky to her friends. It had occurred to him on his way over with his parents that he hadn't seen her in quite some time. Not since long after the birth of her daughter, whose name he couldn't quite recall. *I wonder why she and Mom fell out of touch?* No matter the reason, he hugged the woman he'd called aunt for years and smiled at her with fond remembrance.

"Oh, Amor. How lovely of you to come. It's been absolute ages," Lucky said, clasping his hands warmly and calling him by one of his older names.

"It's actually Maverick now." He couldn't have said what else they talked about because his attention ended up snagged by the curvy shape of a woman setting the table in the dining room to his right.

Shapely and dressed in a form-fitting knit dress, the mystery woman made his cock twitch with interest. Maverick wanted to sigh with relief when he realized that his attraction to Ms. Fortuna was just that, regular old attraction. *And a problem easily solved.*

He didn't struggle or attempt to escape and hide behind his parents when Lucky tugged him toward the woman with the tempting ass. *No time like the present to find a willing partner for a night of hot, satisfying, no-strings-attached sex.*

When the mystery lady whirled, though, to face them, his elation faded, and horror—along with a surge of molten lust—shot through him. "*Roxanne.*" He whispered her name and clenched his fists tightly at his side, fighting an urge to go to her. *I've been set up.*

His damned mother and her matchmaking, He'd thought her done with her games. But looking into Roxanne's startled brown eyes, he couldn't find the enthusiasm to complain.

Apparently, Roxanne felt differently. "Ha, I knew there was no way I could actually want you. You put a spell on me. A love spell with one of your arrows, didn't you? That's why I can't stop thinking of you."

He gaped at her for half a second then laughed. His chuckles grew even louder when she slapped him hard. His cheek took the brunt of the blow, but while she put some force behind it, he didn't flinch. The benefit of being a god. She, however, shook her hand and cursed him.

"Ow! That freaking hurt. You jerk! This is all your fault," she accused him with sparking eyes.

"What is?" He couldn't help but chuckle as she glared at him.

"Dinner. My love life. Or lack of. And my dreams."

She dreams of me? More than ever, the urge to hug her to him grew, and he panicked. "Yeah, well,

I think it's your fault," he snapped back.

"Me?" Her beautiful eyes graced with long lashes widened. "What did I do?"

"Stop looking so damned hot." Maverick wanted to slap himself as soon as he blurted the words out. For whatever reason, he turned into an idiot around her. "I'm going to kill my mother," he muttered.

As Roxanne's cheeks turned a bright red, she muttered, "Funny, I was going to say the same thing of mine."

Maverick's lips twitched, and to his surprise, hers did, too. Seconds later, they were both roaring with laughter.

Roxanne stifled her giggles long enough to ask, "What's your favorite fantasy?"

A wicked grin pulled his lips. "Replacing all my mother's see-through gowns with big flowered muumuus."

She uttered an adorable snicker. "Mine is forging some losing lottery tickets so she thinks she's lost her power."

They both burst into another round of laughter under Lucky's frowning gaze.

"Wicked children," announced his mother, Venus, with a fierce scowl as she joined them.

"Totally disrespectful," agreed Lucky, nodding her head.

"Dinner," announced the blond Viking holding up a platter with a steaming roast.

"Allow me." Manners prevailed. Maverick held out a chair and seated Roxanne, who looked as if she was about to protest. Before she could say anything, he moved around to the other side and seated himself across from her. Not that he had a choice. His parents, along with Roxanne's mother and boyfriend, had commandeered all the other seats.

It occurred to him to just leave instead of forcing himself to endure the torture of her presence, but Maverick just couldn't bring himself to do it. He justified his actions with the fact that nothing could happen surrounded by people and the knowledge Roxanne seemed to not want anything to do with him either. Still, when she studiously avoided looking his way, an annoying fact he noticed, he couldn't help but stare at her. *How did I ever think she was human? Any idiot looking at her can tell she shines with otherness—and sensual beauty.*

He saw her fight the weight of his gaze. Her jaw tightened, as did her fingers around the fork she held. But eventually, her face turned his way and her downcast eyes rose to meet his.

The room and noise around them receded as he found himself focused entirely on her, sucked into the swirling depths of her brown eyes. Her lips trembled, and her cheeks flushed. On his body, it was another part that flushed with blood. The flick of her tongue as she moistened her lips made him harder than he'd imagined possible.

Logic and promises to himself be damned. He wanted this woman. *Now.*

She tore her gaze away, but not before he glimpsed the fear—tempered with longing.

He chewed a dinner tasteless in the face of his rampaging emotions and hormones. He needed to escape before his control slipped his grasp completely and he rushed her to the nearest room to have a taste of her. *Extreme lust, not love.* He repeated this mantra over and over to himself as he sat across from her, aware of her every movement.

How he made it through dinner without going for the dessert he craved was a mystery. His parents and Roxanne's mother seemed oblivious to the undercurrents flying between them. How could they so blithely eat and talk while he struggled against the battering waves of desire that weakened his will and whispered insidiously, *where's the harm in one quick romp?*

Roxanne abruptly stood. "If you'll excuse me, I need to freshen up."

The men, including Maverick, all stood as Roxanne, with a sexy sway of her hips, walked away, her steps getting faster and faster until she dashed into the kitchen and disappeared from sight.

Maverick's brow knitted into a frown. *Hey, wait a second. I don't think she's coming back.*

Irrationality took over his body. He stood. "Um, I need to freshen up as well." He vaguely noticed the smirk on his mother's face matching the one on Lucky's, but before he could analyze their odd looks, he'd already strode away in the same direction as Roxanne.

He quickly walked through the kitchen into a corridor, an empty one. He jogged down the hall, peeking into the open doorways as he passed, not seeing her. A part of him understood his actions had passed into the realm of crazy, but he couldn't stop himself from seeking her out.

At the end of the hall, where the servant's staircase wound up, he caught the flash of a disappearing foot. *Roxanne's or a staff member?* Still not in his right mind, he chased after, climbing the stairs rapidly. Whoever he followed heard him coming, for the footsteps ahead of him broke into a clattering run, and his blood pumping with growing excitement, he gave chase.

At the top of the stairs, he stumbled onto a wide landing and almost missed the closing of a door on silent hinges.

You can't hide from me that easily.

He tiptoed just past the door and plastered himself against the wall. He waited, even as his mind chided him for acting like a mad man, and then waited some more. He listened but heard not even the barest whisper of sound from behind the closed door. But he knew she was in there. He could sense her with every fiber of his being, an odd sensation he chose not to examine.

After several more minutes of languishing outside, he wondered if perhaps he should just barge in when the door opened the barest crack. He flattened himself as the door opened even farther and a familiar head peeked out.

Quicker than a human, he jumped out in front of her and yelled, "Boo!"

Roxanne screamed and plastered a hand to

her chest. "You jerk. What the heck are you doing?"

"Finding out why you're skipping out on dinner," he replied, crossing his arms over his chest.

"I-I—" she stammered as she looked for a lie to feed him.

"I think it's time we tested something," he said, unable to look away from her plump mouth.

"What?" she asked, peering at him with wary eyes.

He didn't answer her. He showed her. Pulling her into his embrace, he folded his arms around her and lowered his head to kiss her.

And at the electrifying touch, he didn't care if he'd lost his mind because, with her in his arms, he found something even better.

Chapter Eight

Roxanne wanted to blame her racing heart on his frightening her. She wanted to excuse the way her blood heated up at his touch on a fever. But as she pressed herself against him, returning his embrace while her hands clutched at his broad shoulders, all she could think of was how right it felt. How wonderful. How exciting.

His hard mouth kissed hers with a passion she'd thought reserved for movies and romance novels. Commanding, yet, at the same time, coaxing. His expertise had her parting her lips to allow a foray by his tongue. In the back of her mind, she knew she should put a stop to this, but the sensuous slide of his tongue against hers… Oh, what a fabulous mistake.

Roxanne sagged in his embrace, which had him tightening his arms around her. A boneless languor had invaded her body at his touch, and while certain parts of her body refused to work—like her legs—other parts of her woke and throbbed, begging for more.

She found herself pushed up against a wall and her skirt riding up to accommodate the thigh pressing between her legs. She ground her cleft against his muscled leg, gasping at the friction this placed on her clit. She heard him suck in a breath before he renewed his sensual exploration by dragging his lips across her cheek to the sensitive shell of her ear. Roxanne couldn't help the moan that slipped from her as her pleasure mounted at his skillful touch.

She thanked the fact that he said not a word. Speaking would have ruined this wondrously erotic moment. Then again, who had time for words when their bodies were so decadently tangled?

She felt his hands slide down her body, skimming over her ruched-up skirt to land his burning touch on the bared skin of her hips. She rotated her pelvis forward, sliding herself on his leg. He got the hint. He slid a finger into the waistband of her panties, stroking a path through her curls to find her nub.

Roxanne hissed in pleasure as he stroked her. Faster and faster he worked her clit while she could only desperately cling to his shoulders, her eyes clamped, shut lest she break the blissful spell they found themselves under. When he stopped his friction to slide that same finger into her damp sex, she mewled, a sound full of longing…and need.

The sound of a zipper had her opening eyes heavy with desire. She gazed down to see his cock spring forth, a long, thick rod straining toward her waiting core. She should protest. Events were moving too fast. She didn't even like him.

Ignoring her rational thoughts, she braced herself with her hands on his shoulders as he used both his hands to hoist her up. She thought to protest, for she well knew she was no lightweight. Her previous boyfriends made no bones of that fact, nor had they ever tried anything so adventurous. But Maverick had no problem with her extra-rounded size, and judging by his turgid shaft, he actually enjoyed it.

The head of his cock probed her wet slit, but instead of impaling her with its length, he finally grunted out a question. "May I?"

Roxanne appreciated his asking, even if his timing sucked. However, so close to the brink, and not caring for the reasons why she shouldn't, she whispered, "Please."

With a groan, he sheathed himself with a solid thrust that made her gasp. Her channel squeezed around his length as he held his deep-seated position inside her. His fingers tightened their grip on her ass cheeks, and thus anchored, he began to move inside her.

It was glorious.

Slowly, he thrust into her, the head of his cock striking a sweet spot inside of her that made her gasp. He increased his pace, his low grunts accompanied by her cries of pleasure.

Never had her body responded so eagerly, or so quickly. Mindless with pleasure, she couldn't halt her keening cries. He caught her mouth with his, his fierce kiss driving her over the brink. She screamed into his mouth as she climaxed hard. The walls of her sex quivered and tightened around him, so snug she felt him as he expanded then spurted hotly inside. And still he continued to plow her, drawing out her orgasm until she thought she would cry with the beauty of it.

Slowly, he stopped his sensual thrusts until he stood still. He buried his face in the soft curve of her neck, his mouth tenderly brushing her skin. She leaned her own head against him, sated and strangely content. It was a perfect moment that, of course, demanded breaking.

"Roxi? Are you up here?"

Roxanne's body stiffened at the sound of her mother's voice calling her from the stairs. "We can't let her find us like this," she whispered as she wiggled in his grasp.

He set her down, his cock slipping wetly from her sex. Roxanne didn't look at him while she jerked down her skirt and kicked her fallen panties under the nearby dresser.

She still hadn't dared peek at him when her mother appeared in the open doorway. *I can't believe we just did that out in the open.* Roxanne wanted to sink into the ground, certain her mother would know what had occurred as soon as she saw them.

Instead, with a bright smile, her mother said, "There you two are. Dessert is being served. Are you coming?"

Roxanne, her cheeks hot and her lips bruised from Maverick's kisses, just about died when he whispered naughtily in her ear, "I think we already came."

Roxanne could do nothing to control the giggles that erupted, a hysterical laughter that had her mother eyeing her strangely.

Hot damn. That man should come with a warning label. Caution: gorgeous, fabulous lover with a sense of humor.

Too bad she intended to never see him again.

Chapter Nine

Maverick, in a much mellower mood than before, took his place at the table after seating Roxanne. *I knew it. All I needed was some great sex to get back to being myself.*

And the sex had truly turned out fantastic. Even rushed and wearing their clothes, he had to admit their passionate coupling certainly earned a top spot where orgasms were concerned. Even better were the blushes that brightened Roxanne's cheeks each time their glances met.

Dessert was served, a light pastry stuffed with a creamy filling and topped with chocolate. Roxanne wrapped her luscious lips around the delicacy and bit down, her eyes closing in enjoyment. Maverick watched her raptly as she devoured the confection with obvious relish. *I wonder if she'd wear the same face while sucking my cock?* Maverick almost blushed at his extremely dirty thought in the presence of not only his parents but her mother as well.

He tried to drag his mind out of the gutter, he truly did, but when the dessert left a creamy spot on her lip, Maverick found himself watching her mouth and waiting. He almost groaned aloud as her pink tongue flicked out and swiped the sweet spot. Inside his pants, his cock showed its thoughts on the matter and thickened.

No, this can't be happening again. I just had her. Why am I so horny already to have her again?

Once again, he set about ignoring her, but she drew him like a magnet, and as if his lust were contagious, he could see her becoming flushed, her eyes glittering brightly. He wondered if anyone would notice if they disappeared again for a few minutes.

When she excused herself, Maverick was only steps behind her. They were no sooner out of sight than he had her pressed up against the wall, hungrily tasting the sweetness that still flavored her mouth.

She kissed him back fervently, but only for a moment before she shoved at him. He drew back, breathing raggedly.

"No. We can't do that again."

The fact that he'd thought the same earlier didn't prevent him from saying, "Why ever not?"

"Because I don't like you, and you don't like me, remember?"

Didn't like her? He pressed himself against her and showed her proof of his *like*. "What's this then?"

Her eyes went slightly unfocused as he ground himself against her. She bit her lip and said a tad breathlessly, "That's lust. And while it was fun, I am not the type of girl to indulge in casual sex."

He looked at her incredulously. "Fun? You

call what we did fun?"

"Okay, it was fantastic. But it can never happen again. I want more out of a man than just sex. I want the whole nine yards, and you can't give it to me."

"Who says it's just sex?" Maverick couldn't believe they were having this conversation—instead of having hot sex. The fact that he'd been determined, just a short while ago, to not get involved didn't enter into his thinking. Lust or love, he didn't really care which one he suffered from. All he knew was he couldn't bear thinking of not seeing or touching her again.

She rolled her eyes. "Um, you're the god of love. Of course it's just sex. Heck, you probably have this effect on all the women you meet. If you think I'm going to let you make me fall in love with you so you can use me and then move on to the next girl, you're crazy. Been there, done that, and I am not interested in a repeat."

She thinks I'm a womanizer? And even more galling, a cheater! That roused his temper. "I'll have you know I have never cheated on anyone I was involved with."

"Ha, but you don't deny being involved with lots of women, do you? See, I'm right. I'd just be another notch in your belt. Well, excuse me, but I'm not interested. Thanks for the sex, it was great, but you'll have to find someone else for a repeat performance."

He wanted to argue that he'd actually only dated rarely in his lifetime. His experience with his ex-wife had left him bitter where love was concerned. But suddenly, a little detail of their coupling came to mind, and he blurted out, "Are you on birth control?"

Her eyes widened in shock and dawning horror. "No. I'm single. Why the heck would I be on the pill? You jerk." She punched him, a blow that didn't hurt him, but she shook her fist, cursing. "Ow! I hate you. I swear, if you impregnated me, I will kill you."

She shoved at him, and Maverick, stunned at the thought she could end up pregnant with his child, let her go. The idea should have horrified him, sent him running, but instead, his heart fluttered and his mind whispered, *I should be so lucky.*

The slamming door woke him from his stupor. He returned alone to the dining area and made excuses for Roxanne's departure before he said his own goodbyes, unable to stay any longer with his mind in such turmoil.

Bemused, he took his leave of his parents and Roxanne's mother, transporting himself back to his penthouse condo. The god of love poured himself a drink and sank onto his leather couch.

A baby? My actual baby? He'd gotten excited before about having a child back when he had been married to Psyche. He'd given in to all his wife's demands and built the forthcoming child the nursery to beat all nurseries. He'd boasted and beamed, his pride over impending fatherhood making him giddy. Then, the child had arrived and he'd held the little bundle, only to realize it wasn't his. And thus did the love spell binding him to his wife start to crumble.

Maverick tossed back the shot, the burning liquid not as hot as the pain of betrayal he'd suffered so long ago. He poured another straight shot of whiskey into his glass and pushed his mind away from his painful past to the present. Or, in other words, Roxanne.

Alone, he could think back over their insane encounter and harden in remembrance. The passionate way she'd responded to him. The soft feel of her against his hands. The molten heat of her core as he claimed her. The fact that he'd lost his mind completely and not even thought of using protection. The way she'd flatly refused considering getting hot and sticky with him again.

Maverick sighed. If there was one consolation in the whole affair it was the fact that his desire for her, and, in return, hers for him, was real. This time, he couldn't blame a mistaken love arrow in his ass, nor could he chalk up her attraction to him as magically induced. Whatever currently transpired between them, while explosive and completely irrational, was the real deal.

It both frightened and elated him. *What if I give in to the feelings swamping me and allow myself to fall in love with her? Can I be sure that this time I won't be hurt?*

His question, oddly enough, mirrored her accusation. She seemed to fear the same thing he did. Betrayal of trust.

His phone rang, and Maverick swallowed the fiery liquor in his glass instead of answering. Somewhat melancholy and introspective, he wasn't ready to talk to anyone right now. Not until he'd figured out what to do next. Actually, he knew what he wanted to do—Roxanne naked on his bed, bent over in his shower, on her hands and knees in the living room. He could think of lots of things he could do with Roxanne that were clothing optional. The question was more of how to convince her she wanted the same.

The phone continued to ring shrilly, and he glanced over to see his mother's number on the call display. He ignored it.

He should have known better.

"Cupie, why aren't you answering your phone?" asked his mother as she materialized in front of him with her hands on her hips.

"Because I'm working on getting drunk," he replied as he refilled his glass.

His mother frowned. "Why? I thought you and Roxanne hit it off. I mean it was kind of obvious the two of you made out when you both left the room—*twice*."

Maverick choked on the whiskey, spitting it out and spattering his mother. She moved to stand behind and whacked him hard between the shoulder blades. With his eyes streaming, he managed to sputter, "You mean you all knew?" Maverick blushed. They'd acted so damned oblivious at the dinner he'd assumed no one had recognized their signs of naughty play. Wrong again.

"Lucky and I are delighted about the fact you guys have decided to get together. It's what we always hoped for."

"Not together," he muttered. "And wait a second, what do you mean, hoped for?" Suspicion formed. "What did you two do?"

His mother wouldn't look him in the eye as she twitched nervously. "We didn't do anything really, well, except for stop the visiting for a few hundred years once Roxanne was born."

Maverick rubbed the bridge of his nose and sighed. "I'm afraid to ask why."

"It's simple. See, after the nasty way Psyche treated you, it occurred to me you needed someone nice. You'd always loved Lucky, so when she had Roxanne, it occurred to us how nice it would be if the two of you got together and fell in love."

"Okay, I get that me getting with the daughter of your good friend would be nice, but why stop seeing Lucky then?" he asked, trying to follow her logic.

"Well, I didn't want you running into Roxanne while she was a child, of course. It's hard to think of someone romantically when you've seen them as a baby pooping in their diaper."

Maverick groaned. "You two are unbelievable. You mean, this whole time, you were both manipulating things in the hopes Roxanne and I would fall in love?"

"I don't know if I'd call it manipulation so much as avoidance until the time was right."

"Yeah, well, you can forget all your little plans. She wants nothing to do with me. She doesn't like me." Maverick said the words almost morosely. What a turnaround from just a day ago.

"What? Why ever not?" his mother asked indignantly. "Doesn't she realize what a catch you are?"

Maverick shrugged. "She seems to think that I'm going to love her and leave her for another."

"That's outrageous," his mother screeched, coming to his defense. "I'll just set her straight then."

Maverick's face blanched in panic. "Don't you dare. This isn't your problem to solve."

"So you have a plan then?"

Maverick rubbed his chin. "Not quite, but I'm not ready to throw in the towel yet. Can I ask you something though, Mom?"

"Anything, Cupie. You know that."

"How did you know Dad was the one?"

His mother's face softened into a smile of remembrance. "Well, other than the fact we couldn't keep our hands off each other, I guess I knew because I just couldn't imagine an eternity without him at my side. When we're apart, I miss him, and when we're together, it just feels right, like he completes me."

Okay, don't freak out. Just because that sounds like what I'm going through doesn't mean it's love. But if it is, and I take a chance, how do I know she feels the same way? An even better question is, am I brave enough to try my luck with love again?

Maverick poured another shot. *Wouldn't my staff at CDS laugh? The god of love afraid of his own specialty.*

Chapter Ten

Roxanne hopped into a shower as soon as she got home from her mother's dinner party—and impromptu shag fest. It wasn't shame that drove her to scrub her skin like a madwoman but the fact that, whenever she caught a whiff of Maverick's scent lingering on her skin, she wanted to kick herself for refusing a second round of riding Cupid's arrow.

Stupid. Insane. Irresponsible. Satisfying. Erotic. No matter how she started castigating herself for allowing him to seduce her—more like pleasure her silly—she always ended up turning in a mental circle where she found herself longing for a repeat.

Her skin pink, if somewhat wrinkled from her extended bathing, she got out of the shower and wrapped a big, fluffy towel around her body. Thus attired, she wandered into her bedroom and screamed.

Venus, who lounged on Roxanne's bed in one of her famous diaphanous gowns, smiled at her and patted a spot beside her on the mattress.

Roxanne clutched her towel tighter. "What are you doing here?"

"I wanted to talk to you about Cupie."

"Who's Cupie?" As soon as she asked,

Roxanne knew and burst out laughing. "Is that what you call Maverick?"

Venus sat up abruptly. "Oh, shoot. Don't tell him I told you that. He'll kill me. He's not too crazy about the nickname."

"I'll bet," Roxanne replied with a snicker. "So, what did you want to tell me about Maverick?" She braced herself for a strict warning about staying away from the god of love. A threat she needed because, even alone, she sensed her resolve crumbling. Heck, she'd already begun thinking of excuses to show up at his office—*and see if his desk is as sturdy as it looks.*

"Maverick hasn't exactly been lucky when it comes to love," Venus said, interrupting yet another naughty thought.

Roxanne snorted as she processed what Venus said. "He's Cupid. How can he not be lucky with women?"

Venus sighed. "You'd think it would be easier for him, but it's the opposite. You only have to take a look at his ex-wife, Psyche."

"What, did she catch him cheating?"

Maverick's mother jumped up off the bed and glared at Roxanne. "My son is not a cheater. He is the most honest, upstanding, loving man a mother or woman could ask for. No, Psyche was the one to betray him. Here's a quick history lesson since you apparently never studied your Greek history like a good demigod daughter. Psyche managed to have Maverick pricked with his own arrow of love, and then she tricked him into marrying her and giving her immortality. That would have been fine, but she never actually loved my poor Cupie. Instead, she cuckolded him under his very nose. Trapped in his own love spell, he didn't suspect a thing until she messed up. She got pregnant by one of her lovers and tried to pass the baby off as his."

Roxanne's mouth snapped shut in shock at the revelation. "But that's just mean."

"Exactly. Initially, Maverick was oblivious to her infidelity, and I am afraid to admit, I was a little too self-involved at the time to notice and do something about it. But when their daughter was born, he couldn't deny the evidence."

Tears pricked Roxanne's eyes. "Oh, he must have been heartbroken." Roxanne's hands slipped to her stomach in reflex.

"He was beyond devastated, especially since the magic of the arrow kept trying to convince him he still loved Psyche, even with the truth of her treachery plain to see. It took him a few hundred years to finally break free of the spell and her, then a few more to divorce the harpy."

"His story is certainly sad, but what does this have to do with me?"

"I saw the way you both looked at each other over dinner, and having slipped off for many a tryst with Ares, I know what you two got up to, as well."

Roxanne blushed. "Um, that was a mistake. We won't be doing that again."

"Why ever not? You both obviously like

each other."

"We're in lust with each other," Roxanne said, her cheeks heating even hotter as she stood in just a towel conversing with the mother of the man she'd gotten intimate with.

"Lust and love. Who's to say where one starts and the other ends? It's how Ares and I began, and now look at us several millennia later."

"But he's a god," Roxanne sputtered. "I don't want to date a god. They're nothing but trouble."

Venus's face fell. "You're still upset about what happened to your father, aren't you? You have to know that not all gods are like him."

"You mean petty and self-centered?" Roxanne asked, arching a brow.

Venus tossed her hair. "Okay, I admit I might have been a tad in my youth, but I, like most others, have grown up."

"Good for you. But I still don't want to get with a god. I like living a mundane life in the human world."

"You sound just like Cupid," Venus said as she wrinkled her nose. "Personally, I don't get it. But, see, it's just one more thing you have in common."

"Does he know you're here?" Roxanne asked with sudden suspicion.

The bright red of her cheeks gave Venus away. "Actually, I kind of promised not to interfere."

"He talked to you about me?" Roxanne

asked, her tone a touch too eager. "Not that I care or anything." Her backtrack came too late, and Venus beamed again.

"See? I knew you liked him. I'm just asking you give him a chance. I promise he's worth the effort."

"I'll think about it." *Yeah, I'll think about it and reject the idea because, no matter what you say, I don't for one minute think Cupid, the god of love, is actually going to fall in love with a demigoddess with wide hips and a plump ass. Even if he did seem to enjoy grabbing it.*

Gorgeous gods like Maverick, while dallying with the plainer, plump maidens, always ended up marrying the beautiful, graceful type. And as she knew from experience, even when a man professed love, the first sign of a come-hither glance and they were off sniffing and mowing greener pastures.

At least her vague answer satisfied Venus who, with a thumbs-up and a smile, disappeared back to Olympus where she lived.

Roxanne peered around to make sure she was alone then dropped her towel. She hadn't even shimmied on her undies when the phone rang.

Sighing, she sat down and answered. "Hello, Mother."

"Roxi, baby. You left so abruptly I wanted to make sure everything was all right. Are you *busy*?"

"I'm fine. I just wanted to get to bed early. Big day at the office tomorrow," she lied.

"Oh. You don't have company?" Lucky queried.

"No. Why would you think that?"

"Well, the way you and Maverick got on and both left so quickly made me think you'd made plans to meet."

Roxanne closed her eyes and held in another sigh. "Not you too. Listen, like I just told your pal, Venus, I am not getting involved with a god. I don't care how handsome or nice he is. It's not worth the heartache."

"Oh."

Roxanne listened as the scratching sound of someone covering the mouthpiece came through loud and clear. "Oh bother," she muttered, hugging the phone between her ear and shoulder as she dug out some worn, cotton jammies. She'd just managed to pull the bottoms up, her chest still bare, when her mother came back on the line.

"Listen, I'll call you tomorrow," her mother said. "Bye."

A click and dial toned filled the air. Roxanne shook her head at her mother's odd phone call. It might have ended abruptly, but at least she could now finish dressing.

Barely, for she'd no sooner poked her head through the hole of the top than the phone rang again.

Expecting her mother again, her tone came out harried when she answered with a brusque, "What now?"

"Um, dinner?" questioned a velvety male voice that had her sitting down hard on her bed.

"Maverick?" Her heart sped up.

"Hi. Sorry to call so late, but I wanted to ask you out for dinner."

"Why? Did your mother put you up to this?" she asked with suspicion.

"Please tell me my mother didn't visit you?"

"In the flesh. She wants me to date you."

She smiled as she heard him groaning. "I'm going to kill her. Listen, ignore anything she said, unless you liked it of course, and say you'll have dinner with me."

"Why?"

"Honestly, I want to get to know you better."

Roxanne knew the right thing to say was no, but instead, she replied, "Yes."

His voice seemed brighter. "Great. I'll pick you up at seven tomorrow night. Dream of me." He hung up with those huskily spoken words, and Roxanne flopped back onto her bed.

What am I thinking? Going to dinner with him. I know where that's going to end up.

With her enjoying another fabulous orgasm probably. But she couldn't muster the enthusiasm to be angry about it, and as he commanded, she dreamt of him, all night long.

Chapter Eleven

Roxanne couldn't concentrate the following day at work and, as a result, made a few bad stock choices. By her third money losing trade, she gave up and went home to prepare for her date.

Much as it irritated her, and even though it made her seem like a teenage girl with a crush, she couldn't help the anticipation that thrummed through her. She'd tried countless times since his phone call the previous night to convince herself the date was a stupid idea. She'd told herself numerous times to call and cancel. She swore a vow to herself that all he'd get was dinner, the off-the-plate kind, and not a taste of her pie, even as she shaved her pubes almost clean.

Who am I kidding? I want to see him, and I want him to touch me and lick me and do all kinds of naughty things to my body.

At seven on the nose, a knock sounded at her door, and dressed in her seventh outfit—a form-fitting black cocktail dress with an easy access skirt covering her G-string—she took a deep breath before answering.

He looked delicious dressed in a dark blue suit that made his blue eyes appear brighter. He thrust something at her, and she automatically reached out to grab it, expecting flowers. Instead, she grasped cold metal.

What the heck? She looked down in bafflement at the contraption she held consisting of metal bands and a lock. "What is it?" she asked, confusion creasing her brow.

"A chastity belt. I need you to put it on."

Roxanne snorted. "Seriously? Why would I do that?"

In seconds, he'd pressed her up against the wall and his hungry lips had found hers. Roxanne didn't remain stunned long. She flung her arms around his neck, almost braining him with the medieval contraption. But in the grips of instant desire, she didn't care, and she returned his kiss with the same ferocity. For several minutes, their mouths became reacquainted, and the fire, which had smoldered in her cleft all day, sprang up with a liquid heat that dampened her thighs.

Maverick pulled away with evident reluctance, his hard body moving away from hers. Roxanne mewled softly in loss before opening her eyes. She didn't immediately see Maverick because he'd moved well out of reach, but she noted his agitation as he ran a hand through his blonde curls, rumpling them.

"Now do you see why you need to put it on?" he exclaimed. "We'll never make it through dinner otherwise. Hell, we won't even make it to the restaurant at this rate."

Roxanne, wet and horny, gave him a lazy smile. "So, let's go straight to dessert then." Her wanton words, at odds with her earlier thoughts, flowed easily from her mouth. Even more shocking, she meant them. Knowing he couldn't control himself around her was a heady, powerful feeling. It made her feel desirable and, despite her lusher frame...*sexy.*

Something in her look made him back away and raise his hands defensively before him. "Stop looking at me like that, Roxanne. I only have so much control, and you are really testing it. And much as I'd love to feast on your succulent skin..." Maverick swallowed hard, and his eyes went slightly out of focus. "What was I saying? Ah yes, I want us to go have dinner like two normal people getting to know each other. So put the damned thing on so I can stop thinking of how I'd like to dive under that skirt and find out firsthand what color your panties are."

"Who says I'm wearing any?" she replied impishly. Despite her resolutions, the darned man made it hard not to like him. Even better, he seemed determined to get to know her, and not in a carnal sense. *What a shame.*

He groaned and closed his eyes. "Don't torture me. Just go put the chastity belt on."

Roxanne grinned as she went into her bedroom to comply. Truth told the idea of wearing it kind of excited her. Knowing he couldn't touch her actually heightening her arousal. But he was right—without it, they probably wouldn't make it out the door. She also discovered that, despite her earlier vehemence about not dating a god, she wanted to find out more about him. Discover what kind of man he truly was, and if they were as compatible emotionally as they seemed to be physically.

It took Roxanne a few minutes to figure out the darned belt. Eventually, she managed to step into it and yank it into place around her pelvis. Imbued with magic of some sort, the metal molded comfortably to her body and prevented all access to her cleft. It was only after she locked it into place with the provided key that she wondered how she'd pee.

Given the magical nature of the device, she had to assume the designer had taken bodily functions into account. Smoothing her dress back down, she sashayed back into her living room, where Maverick paced.

"Did you lock it up?" he asked, his tone anxious.

Roxanne dangled the key.

He snatched it and strode into her kitchen. She followed and watched as he dropped it into a glass of water and slid it in the freezer.

"How's that supposed to help?" she asked.

"One thing I can't do is call heat," he said with a shrug. "So I've got plenty of time to regain control of myself before the ice melts and I ravish you."

"What if I want you to ravish me?" she teased. For some reason, she felt at ease enough with him to joke, and she enjoyed it. Judging by the twinkle in his eye, so did he.

"I want you to want more than just my body," he replied as he tucked her hand into the crook of his arm.

Roxanne blushed. "I'm sorry. You bring out the wanton in me. I swear I'm not usually like this."

He dropped a light kiss on her lips. "I didn't say I didn't enjoy it. I do. Now that we've contained our insane lust for each other, why don't we find out if we have anything else in common other than meddling mothers?"

Uncanny, the way he seemed to mirror her thoughts, and as Roxanne followed Maverick out into the night to his waiting car, she actually wished—even though he was a dreaded god—that they would find mutual ground.

Because I've never felt like this before, and even scarier, I don't want it to end.

Chapter Twelve

Maverick couldn't help himself from touching Roxanne. She looked so beautiful sitting beside him in the restaurant, her generous curves deliciously displayed in a form-fitting dress. She'd swept her long hair up, exposing the graceful line of her neck. He liked that she wore only a light coating of makeup, allowing her natural beauty to shine through. She fascinated and drew him like he'd never imagined anyone doing, not without some kind of magical aid.

After they'd ordered, it seemed natural for him to grab her hand and hold it. After a moment's hesitation, she curled her fingers around his and his heart swelled.

The previous evening's talk with this mother had made him realize he had to explore his burgeoning feelings for Roxanne, hence the dinner invitation. The chastity belt had actually been a clever idea of his father, whom he talked to earlier that day. When he'd asked Ares how to prove Roxanne he wanted more from her than just her body, his father suggested making her body off-limits. Given Maverick's lack of control around her, the chastity belt, while medieval, seemed ideal. Maverick wanted, make that needed, to show

Roxanne that he was serious about getting to know her and not just how she looked naked—although he hoped to enjoy that knowledge in the near future.

Dinner passed in a pleasant blur as, slowly, they learned about each other. They exchanged life stories, the only low point coming when he asked about her father. The story of her father's death at the hands of a petty god made Maverick want to hunt the perpetrator down and kill him for hurting her. It also made him understand her reluctance to get involved with a god, a reluctance he planned to overcome. In the spirit of honest exchange, he told her about his marriage to Psyche.

She admitted his mother had revealed the ugly truth to her, but as she said with a smile and shrug, "Having been cheated on by more than one boyfriend, I can totally understand the pain."

With their skeletons out of the closet so to speak, they grew more and more relaxed. To his surprise, Maverick noticed that, while his attraction for her was ever present, his fascination with her as a person made it easy to control his lusty thoughts. *What do you know? I find her mind just as intriguing as her body.*

As the evening drew on and they finished their dinner, they discovered more and more things in common. They both enjoyed action movies, loved to ski, and, if they had to choose any animal in the world as a pet, would go with a turtle.

They were laughing over coffees when a shadow fell over them. A cloud of perfume tickled his nose, and Maverick's stomach sank as a familiar icy voice interrupted his date.

"Amor, what a pleasure to run into you."

Maverick didn't bother standing and only spared a brief glance at Psyche, his ex-wife. "Hello, Psyche. I wish I could say the same."

As far as he was concerned, he'd prefer never to see her again. While some men might have spent more time staring at the slim, statuesque blonde, the term ice princess aptly described not only Psyche's looks but personality as well.

A moue of annoyance curled her lips, and Maverick almost groaned as he saw Psyche's gaze flick over at Roxanne, whose hand he still firmly held.

"I see you've found a new body to stick your arrow in. Really, Amor, your standards have slipped. If you're that desperate to get laid, you could have called. I would have taken care of you for old time's sake."

Maverick flushed with anger and prepared to retort, but Roxanne beat him to it. "So this is the skank you were married to?" Roxanne eyed Psyche up and down and shook her head. "Wow, that must have been one powerful spell to ever make you want Miss High Maintenance over there. Anyone can see she's got bitch written all over her."

A blotchy red stained Psyche's cheeks and she sputtered, "No one talks to me like that. You've just bought yourself a whole lot of trouble."

"Screw with me and you'll spend eternity cursing your bad luck," Roxanne replied sweetly, her annoyance betrayed only by her flashing eyes.

Maverick grinned and stroked Roxanne's hand with the pad of his thumb. "Go spew your venom elsewhere, Psyche. We're not interested."

Psyche's face twisted into an ugly rictus, but instead of lashing out with more venomous words, she spun on her heel and walked away.

"Sorry about that," Maverick apologized.

"Don't you dare be sorry," Roxanne replied angrily. "You did nothing wrong. She's just a nasty piece of work. Thank goodness you broke the love spell chaining you to her. But I have to ask. I thought that was impossible? I mean, once shot with one of your Cupid arrows, isn't the love supposed to be forever?"

"Usually. I'm still not sure how I escaped. I mean, even after I found out she'd betrayed me, I still had a hard time breaking free."

"And now when you see her?"

Maverick could hear the unspoken question. "The only thing I feel for Psyche is disgust. If I wasn't so fond of her daughter, I'd have killed her a long time ago for her treachery."

"Do you like kids?"

She asked the question with hesitance, and Maverick hastened to reassure her. "I love children and hope to have my own someday. Even though Bliss wasn't my actual daughter, I've always doted on her. What about you, how do you feel about motherhood?"

"I'd love to have a family with the right man," she said, boldly meeting his gaze. When he didn't flinch, she blushed. "But when I do, I want to raise them in the mortal world, away from the games of the gods."

Thus did they embark on a discussion of the things they preferred in the mortal realm versus the playground of the gods, a discussion that followed them as he drove her home.

He pulled up in front of her place, and the sexual magnetism that they'd managed to keep on a low simmer as they got to know each other flared to life. He helped her from the car, and in silence for the first time since the evening started, he escorted her upstairs.

The air sizzled between them, and he could see her mounting anticipation in the flush of her cheeks and her smoky gaze. They'd no sooner entered the privacy of the elevator than they fell on each other, their mouths meeting with fiery result.

Maverick pressed her against the wall of the cab and plunged his tongue into her mouth to hotly duel with hers. In seconds, they were both panting, and he loved the feel of her fingers digging into his shoulders as she pressed herself against him with sweet gasps of pleasure.

The dinging sound announcing their arrival to her floor interrupted their frantic necking. She led the way with a come-hither glance over her shoulder. Maverick followed, the lure of her shapely ass more potent than any siren's song.

Roxanne opened her apartment door with

her key. She stepped in and turned to look back at him when he didn't follow. "Aren't you coming in?" Her sultry tone and sensuous smile made it clear she expected him to.

However, Maverick had realized something as they connected over dinner—*I'm in love.* Despite the shortness of their meeting, despite the fact that they'd gotten off on the wrong foot, he was completely and utterly in love with Roxanne. The knowledge almost blew him away. Even given his status as god of love, he'd always scoffed at the concept of love at first sight because he knew better. Love at first sight was simply the effect of one of his arrows.

But this...what Roxanne evoked in him since their first meeting... It was more powerful and humbling than he'd ever imagined. It also made him rashly admit, "I want to, but just so you know, if I make love to you tonight, I'm never going to let you go. I love you, Roxanne."

Chapter Thirteen

Roxanne could only stare at Maverick, stunned at his declaration. Her first panicked impulse was to slam the door shut in his face because, despite her warnings to herself, she loved him too. To hear him say the words first, though, to declare he wanted her not just for tonight but forever...

She threw her arms around his neck and showed him with actions instead of words what she thought of his promise.

Entwined, they tumbled into her apartment, the door slamming shut behind them as they frantically resumed their passionate embrace. Blissful heat raced through her body as all of her nerve endings woke and tingled. His hands seemed to be everywhere, stroking her flesh through the thin silk of her dress, his fingers brushing over her nipples already hardened into points. Her hands were equally busy, tracing the strong shape of his shoulders and arms, her tongue sensually stroking his. Panty-wetting desire made her impatient, and she tugged at the buttons on his shirt. In her haste, some of the buttons pinged off.

He laughed softly and grabbed her hands, pulling them above her head to trap them.

"Impatient little minx."

Roxanne's cheeks flushed, but more because of the smoldering heat in this gaze than embarrassment over her destruction of his shirt. With her hands caught by his, she was very aware of being at his mercy. Small tugs didn't budge them, and his evident strength excited her.

"What do you want?" he asked huskily.

"You," she replied. Her lips curved into a mischievous smile. "Naked preferably."

He groaned and dipped his head to kiss her, a soft embrace that had her sighing in his mouth. The thrust of his thigh between her legs reminded her of one very important fact.

"Um, Maverick," she panted. "I think you forgot something."

"Ah, yes. My minx wanted me naked."

Actually, she'd intended to remind him of the key for the chastity belt still sitting in her freezer. But she forgot that thought when he released her and stepped back, the glimpse of his bare chest through the front of his shirt where she'd popped the buttons teasing her.

His lips quirked as he grasped his shirt with two hands and tore it from his body. Roxanne had to lean back against the wall for support, her whole body trembling in excitement and anticipation.

Magnificent. It was the only word to describe his upper body, which rippled with muscles and had the yummiest abs she'd ever seen on a man.

She licked her lips. "More. Show me all of you."

His eyes flashed, but he complied, a quick flick of his wrist undoing the button of his pants. The erection tenting his crotch sprang forth through the opening, riveting her. He let his dress slacks fall, but her eyes, caught by his bobbing cock, barely noted his muscular thighs and tight balls.

"Your turn to strip."

Startled, Roxanne raised her eyes to his. "But—"

"Or would you prefer I rip your clothes off you?" he asked with a teasing smile.

Roxanne's breath hitched—*oh my, that sounds exciting*. Maverick caught the sound. He growled, and in a flash, he was in front of her. His strong hands ripped the material of her dress into two halves, which fluttered to the floor leaving her clad only in her brassiere and the chastity belt. Roxanne trembled with lust.

His eyes took her in from the overflowing cleavage spilling from her lace bra to the roundness of her belly. A frown knitted his brow as his gaze dropped lower.

"Dammit." Naked, he strode off in her kitchen, his firm buttocks a delight to behold. In moments, he'd returned with the glass containing the frozen ice and the key.

"Where's your microwave?" he demanded.

Roxanne shrugged. "Broken. I keep forgetting to buy a new one."

Maverick sighed. "I guess we have to wait."

He looked so forlorn that Roxanne had to

laugh. "You mean I need to wait for my turn, which is just fine by me." She placed her hands on his bare chest, the sizzling contact of her skin against his a prelude for the full-body contact she planned for later. She pushed him backwards toward her couch.

His eyes narrowed. "What are you doing?"

"Getting you in position so I can suck your cock," she replied brazenly.

"But the ice—" he stammered.

"Will melt, I'm sure, eventually. In the meantime, you're going to sit." She shoved at him and toppled him onto the couch. "And enjoy what I'm going to do to you. Don't worry. Once that ice melts, I intend to get my turn."

Maverick clutched the frozen glass, his eyes smoldering as she knelt between his legs, bringing her eye-to-eye with his jutting cock. A good size, she liked the way his shaft curved, the marble of its head glistening with moisture. She dragged a finger up the underside of his rod, watching in fascination as his sac drew up tight. She wrapped her fingers around the base of him, enjoying the thickness and heat. Leaning forward, she darted out her tongue to lap at his mushroom head. Sweet 'n' salty, the taste of him made her smile, especially when she heard him suck in a breath. The cap of his shaft popped into her mouth, and she swirled her tongue around him before taking her mouth down his turgid length. He made a choking sound. She released her hand from his base and took him deeper as she flicked her gaze up to see his face.

He looked in agony, his face taut with strain, his eyes tightly closed. As if sensing her stare, he opened his eyes and turned his burning gaze on her, the heat of it stroking her and making her sex clench. Eyes locked, she sucked him, her cheeks hollowing as she pulled on his cock with her wet mouth. She loved the way he fought to control himself. His ragged breathing and escaping grunts showed her just how hard he strove against coming. *That won't do at all.*

She grabbed his balls with one hand, squeezing and rolling them between her fingers. He hissed in pleasure, and she renewed her sucking efforts as she fondled him. Moisture lubed her fingers on his sac, and she wondered at its source but not for long. The god of love might not have been able to generate magical heat, but apparently, he threw off more than enough of the sexual kind. His hands gripped the frozen glass tightly, and it was from this the water dripped to roll down into his groin. At this rate, it wouldn't take much longer for her turn to arrive.

She couldn't wait.

Drawing her mouth up the length of him, she let him feel the edge of her teeth, a rigid friction on his tender skin that made him shout her name. "Roxanne!"

She squeezed his balls and, through the swollen head in her mouth, said, "Come for me, Let me taste you on my tongue." Her dirty words acted as the catalyst to her actions. With a bellow and a cracking sound as he crushed the glass, he came in a hot torrent in her mouth. She took what he offered and swallowed it, her mouth sucking his tender head, drawing out his pleasure.

"Enough," he panted.

Roxanne released his sated shaft with a popping sound and smiled up at him. He grinned back at her.

"Have I told you yet how amazing you are?" he asked.

"I'd prefer you showed me," Roxanne replied impishly.

"Oh, I intend to," he promised, holding up the freed key.

Roxanne's breath hitched as she realized her turn had arrived. She hadn't even finished that thought when she found herself being carried in his arms in the direction of her bedroom.

"Don't you need time to recover?" she asked as she twined her arms around his neck.

"I'm a god. I can go all night long."

And with those eye-opening words, he dropped her on the mattress.

On her back, she could only look up at him, his beautifully built body and the already semi-hard cock pointing at her. He knelt on the bed between her legs, his hands fumbling the key into the lock of the chastity belt. It had no sooner opened than he tugged it off her and sent it flying across the room.

Roxanne blushed at the way his eyes hungrily devoured her exposed sex, especially when she felt the warm moisture seeping between her nether lips.

"Mmm, my turn," he growled before covering her.

Chapter Fourteen

Maverick could hardly think straight, so consumed did he find himself with Roxanne. It blew his mind—and his cock—that she'd so enthusiastically pleasured him, and very well at that. He needed to return that favor, plus some.

First, though, he visually took her in. He'd loved her rounded shape when she was dressed, but her nakedness left him awed. Skin smooth and clear as fine porcelain, she looked good enough to eat—*and I will feast on her.*

He freed her large, plush breasts from the confines of her bra, his already hardening cock bobbing at the sight of her puckered nipples. Her freed pussy beckoned him with the scent of her arousal and welcoming moisture.

So much for him to explore. He didn't know where to start.

Roxanne licked her lips and looked at him through heavy-lidded eyes. He covered her body with his, the softness of her frame the perfect complement to his harder one. He was careful to keep his full weight off her, but she had other ideas. Her arms twined around his neck, yanking on him.

The little minx still thought to control the

action. *She had her turn, though. Now it's mine.*

Maverick caught her bottom lip between his teeth and tugged it. She squirmed under him, her hips thrusting up to press her mound against him.

If she continued her impassioned pleas with her body, he'd never have the strength of will to explore her properly. *And I really want to discover every inch of her. What makes her sigh, the touches that make her moan, the sensitive spots that make her cream.*

He untangled her arms from around his neck and pushed them over her head. As before, when he'd manhandled her in this method, she flushed and moaned. Roxanne could act tough all she wanted in public. In private, she liked it when he took control.

Anchoring her hands with one of his, he commenced exploring. He kissed her briefly before moving his mouth to the sensitive skin of her neck, hotly sucking her, the urge to leave his mark on her strong. But there were better places to leave a hickey, private places.

He slid his mouth down to the valley between her breasts, burying his face. His free hand cupped one of the heavy globes, squeezing its plentiful handful. He lifted his head, only far enough to grab her protruding nipple. He latched onto it, sucking and swirling his tongue around the tip as she writhed and mewled.

He stopped his oral torture just long enough to blow on the nub. She arched her chest, her cry the sweetest sound. He moved his attention to the other nipple, lavishing upon it the same attention, but a little more forcefully at her mumbled urging. He could have toyed with her breasts all day, their sensitivity making his play with them so enjoyable.

But her thrusting hips, and the dampness connecting with his skin, kept reminding him of the treasures still waiting to be found. His tongue couldn't wait.

He slid down her body, his hand still gripping hers but pulling them down to accommodate his new objective.

She went still as his lips brushed the top of her pubes. He nuzzled her, the scent of her arousal strong and heady. Without any urging on his part, she parted her legs farther and drew up her knees, exposing her beautiful pink shell to him.

He blew warmly on her moist flesh, which quivered.

"Maverick," she moaned.

The way she said his name sent a shiver throughout him. He'd pleasured women before, but no one had ever made him feel like Roxanne did. Like he would lose control. Like he would die if he didn't taste her.

He'd meant to tease her longer, but he couldn't resist the perfume of her arousal, a sensual sweetness that begged to be tasted. He opened his mouth and placed it on her pussy. She bucked hard, dislodging him.

Maverick finally let go of her hands to use both of his to anchor her hips. Pinned, she could only cry out as his tongue traced the trembling lips of her sex. Her hands, now free, gripped his hair, the painful tugging a pleasure of its own because it meant he was giving her a return on the bliss she'd given him.

His mouth and tongue explored her, the taste of her nectar a sweet ambrosia that made him almost frantic with haste. He forced himself to slow down, rubbing his tongue along the length of her slit up to her clit. Swollen with need, her nub beckoned him. He flicked his tongue back and forth on it.

It was too much for Roxanne, whose body was already too sensitized. She screamed as she came, and Maverick plunged his tongue between her wet folds to enjoy the tremors of her orgasm. Her first orgasm.

When her keening cries and shaking slowed down, he went back to working her clit. She shook and gasped as he stroked her ebbing pleasure, rebuilding it to the point where she was yanking on his hair as if she'd scalp him.

"Please." She moaned the word, and Maverick heard her need, a need he felt, as well.

He slid up her body until he covered her. He braced himself on his forearms as the tip of his cock found her welcoming sex. He'd no sooner begun edging his way into that snug haven than she locked her legs around him, pulling him in.

Maverick closed his eyes at the intense sensation. Tight, wet, and still slightly quivering, her channel made him want to lose control and pound her flesh, a race for the release he sensed hovering close by.

But he wanted her to come with him when he did. Gritting his teeth, he fought the waves of pleasure engulfing him to move inside her slowly, thrusting and receding. The tip of his cock butted up against her sweet spot, a strike that caused her to tighten around him. The sensation was beyond exquisite. Her hands reached to cup his face, drawing him down for a passionate kiss that urged him to move faster.

Their bodies moving in rhythm, he lost himself in the sensual softness of her body, her panting cries urging him on and on. The moment of her climax was unmistakable. Her keening scream accompanied by the clenching of her sex around his shaft. A wet, quivering grip that he could not resist. A final thrust to the hilt and he spurted hotly inside her, the racking shudders of his orgasm making him throw his head back to bellow her name.

The bliss took so long to die down that it seemed to last forever. Fine by him. When his body finally loosened into limp satiation, he opened his eyes and smiled down at her.

He found her regarding him with an expression akin to wonder. Her flushed cheeks, bright eyes, and swollen lips were the most attractive things he'd ever seen.

He uttered the words that sang in his heart. "I love you."

Chapter Fifteen

Maverick looked at her expectantly, and Roxanne wanted to say the words, but once she put them out there, once she declared herself hopelessly in love, she gave him the power to hurt her.

Even if I don't think he would. Fear of ruining this moment, this beautiful beginning, made her hesitate. And the moment to speak passed.

She could see the shadow of disappointment in his eyes, even though he didn't voice it aloud. Instead, he brushed her lips tenderly with his. He then rolled to his side and tucked her into him, his strong arms wrapping around her protectively.

"I'm sorry," she whispered, feeling she'd let him down.

He squeezed her. "Don't be. You might not be able to say it yet, but I know how you feel. I am the god of love, after all. But believe me when I say I love you. I'll never hurt or betray you. That, I promise. And I intend to show you just how much you mean to me every day for the rest of our lives, which, given our parentage, will probably be quite lengthy."

Roxanne's eyes misted. Such a dear, wonderful man. *How stupid am I to hold back when he's bared himself to me?* In the past, she'd never had a problem saying the L word. And, like a curse, as soon as she'd uttered it, she'd gotten shafted. Although, if she were to admit it to herself, she'd never actually loved any of those men, not like she did Maverick. Since the moment she'd met him, he'd captured her attention and taken a piece of her heart. In his arms, she felt whole and, even stranger, like she'd come home.

I need to stop being such a ninny and tell him. She would have to, except she realized during her inner chat with herself that he'd fallen asleep.

I'll tell him tomorrow, she promised herself.

Except the following morn, the right moment never arrived. Between her mother calling to demand details on her date and sleepover—*gods just have to know everything, especially mommy ones*—his office paging, and the quickie that left her sticky and needing a shower, they both rushed off to work. She could have probably told him in between the kisses in the elevator on the way down, but quite frankly, all thought fled her mind when he groped under her skirt to steal her panties. "A token," he'd called it, with her scent so that he could relive their pleasure throughout the day. *Incorrigible and adorable.* She'd driven to her office with a smile on her face.

But once she reached work, she couldn't stop thinking of him. Of imagining the delight on his face when she told him the words he longed to hear. The pleasure he'd show her in return.

What the heck am I waiting for? I'm obviously not

going to get any work done, so I might as well go find him and tell him what's in my heart.

The solution seemed so simple. As she jumped in her car to drive over to his office—their first meeting place—to surprise him, she couldn't help the grin on her face. After all, their relationship had begun with her trying to discredit Cupid, only to find out screwing Cupid was what she really needed.

Chapter Sixteen

"I'm leaving for the day," Maverick announced to Mrs. Pettibone as he walked out of his office.

"You? Leaving early?" Mrs. Pettibone clutched her chest in mock disbelief.

Maverick laughed at her antics. He'd found himself in a buoyant mood all day, and he had one woman to thank for that—Roxanne. The woman of his dreams. The one meant to be by his side for eternity. Every second away from her ticked interminably. She apparently felt the same way, too, even if she couldn't say the words, because his receptionist in the main lobby had just buzzed him to say Roxanne waited downstairs for him.

Maverick, who'd pulled her panties out every so often for an eye-closed whiff that brought to life the previous night, dropped everything in his rush to see her. "I've got a hot date with the most wonderful woman in the world," he told his receptionist with a wink as the elevator doors slid open. "And if I'm lucky, she'll soon agree to be my wife."

He laughed at the round 'O' of surprise on Mrs. Pettibone's face. Her exclaimed, "Who is she?" was cut off by the closing doors. Maverick was still grinning when the elevator doors opened and he saw Roxanne talking animatedly with Lisa. The radiant smile she turned on him warmed him more than the fires of Hell—his father's second home.

Maverick sauntered toward her, trying not to run and make a complete ass of himself in front of his employee. As god of love, he did need to keep up appearances, after all, even if his love for Roxanne made him want to act like a rash schoolboy.

A cool breeze fluttered over his skin and sent a sudden chill through him. He turned his head to see Psyche appear with an icy smile.

"Amor, where are you off to looking like an eager puppy?"

"Go away. I've got plans," he replied tersely, turning away from his ex-wife, not in the mood for her antics.

Psyche, however, wouldn't allow him to dismiss her so easily. She grabbed him by the arm and halted him. "Plans with the heifer? Not anymore," she said with a smirk.

The cattiness of her tone made Maverick frown. "Stay away from Roxanne. You already messed my love life up once. I'll kill you before I let you screw it up again."

"Too late." Psyche's triumphant laughter made him turn to check on Roxanne, who had turned away from Lisa to face a man entering the edifice's main doors.

"That's her ex-boyfriend, Kyle," Psyche

announced at his side. "Poor sap, she dumped him just because he cheated on her in her own bed. But don't worry. He's about to get the reunion he's been dying for."

Maverick never saw who shot the arrow, one of his *special* arrows. Even with all his godly speed and powers, he couldn't reach Roxanne before the missile found its mark in the plump flesh of her ass. But he tried anyways, moving in a blur of speed while, at the same time, yelling, "No!"

Too late.

His step slowed and his heart stuttered. Pain constricted his chest as the woman he loved turned to face her ex-boyfriend and he realized he couldn't do a thing to prevent her from becoming a victim of love's curse.

He saw her stiffen, probably in shock as her heart and mind suddenly realized—if falsely—that she was in love with Kyle, the first man she laid eyes on after the direct hit.

Psyche, in the running for the award for most evil bitch, had the balls to come stand by him and laugh. "That'll teach you to snub me."

Maverick skirted his ex-wife and headed toward Roxanne, dreading what he knew would happen but at the same time unable to stop himself from facing her one last time.

One last time before she told him she no longer loved him but wanted to return to her cheating ex-boyfriend.

Who do I, the god of love, pray to when love has

forsaken me?

Chapter Seventeen

Roxanne restrained an urge to rub her ass cheek. Oddly enough, it had felt as if someone had poked her with a needle, which was crazy considering she was waiting in the CDS vestibule. Even crazier was the familiar face walking toward her.

"Roxi, someone told me I could find you here. Isn't it just fate that we should both meet up at the company that introduced us?" Kyle beamed at her.

A heavy left her. "Kyle, you're an idiot. Go away. I'm meeting someone."

"But Roxi," he said with a whine in his voice that made her grind her teeth. "I came all this way to tell you I love you and that I'm sorry. So, what do you say? Wanna give it another go?"

Roxanne drew up all of her five-foot-nine inches—plus two inches in heels—and in her iciest tone replied, "Kyle, if you were the last man alive, I'd kill myself rather than get back with you. Now go away before my boyfriend gets here."

Strong arms wrapped around her from behind, and Roxanne leaned back into the warm, comforting presence of Maverick. "Want me to beat him up?" he whispered in her ear, sounding oddly choked.

"Can't you make him fall in love with a shrew instead?" Roxanne replied, bringing her hands to rest over Maverick's.

"I know just the one." His chuckle, deep and low, next to her ear made her shiver deliciously.

Kyle frowned at them. "You're dating the suit?"

"Correction. I'm mad for the guy in the suit. And now, if you'll excuse us, we need to go."

But instead of marching out the front doors, Roxanne found herself twirled around and, with Maverick's arm firmly anchored around her waist, towed back in the direction of the elevator.

"Did you forget something in your office?" she asked as they stepped into the cab.

The doors slid shut, and she found herself pressed up against the wall with Maverick's eyes smoldering down at her. "Do you have any idea how special you are?"

Roxanne smiled and wrapped her arms around his neck. "Care to show me?"

He granted her wish with a speed that sucked her breath away, his hard lips slanting over hers in a possessive kiss that left her weak-kneed. When his hands began pushing at her skirt, Roxanne, with what little mind she had left, exclaimed, "We can't do this here. The doors could open any second."

Maverick slapped his hand sideways on the red emergency stop button. The elevator shuddered to a halt.

At first, Roxanne gaped at him, then giggled. He silenced her with a kiss and resumed tugging up her skirt.

She found herself just as eager to touch him, her excitement fueled in part by their location. She ripped a few buttons in her haste to feel his skin.

Maverick chuckled. "Minx. I see I'm going to have to put a tailor on retainer if I'm going to have anything to wear."

Roxanne would have blushed, but instead, she cried out as his hands under her skirt discovered her still pantyless state. She closed her eyes in bliss as he stroked her, his fingers alternately rubbing her clit and delving within her damp folds.

A crackling sound was followed by a tinny voice coming from a speaker above them. "Don't worry, Mr. Eros. We'll get you and your lady friend out of there in a few minutes. Hang tight."

Roxanne froze and then erupted into laughter.

Maverick ruefully smiled down at her as he tugged her skirt back down. "I guess we'll have to wait for a night when we've got the building to ourselves to baptize the elevator."

"I can't wait," she said, leaning up to kiss him.

Maverick held her hand firmly as the elevator finished its ascent to the penthouse office. When they stepped out together to his widely grinning receptionist, Roxanne blushed, especially when Mrs. Pettibone said, "I guess we don't need maintenance after all."

To the sound of her laughter, they fled to his office. Once inside the private room, Roxanne paced the wide confines as he stripped off his shirt with the torn buttons and pulled out a fresh one from a closet he kept. Running her hand over the polished surface of his desk, a naughty thought inspired her.

In seconds, she'd hopped up on the top and, using her huskiest voice, said, *"Maverick."*

"What is—" He turned and froze as she pulled her skirt up and leaned back on her elbows.

"I've got a fantasy," she admitted. "Care to guess what it is?"

As it turned out, he shared the same desire. In moments, their passion reignited, she clung to him with wild abandon as he pistoned between her thighs, his mouth capturing her enthusiastic cries. Her orgasm hit her fast and hard, her shudders seemingly never ending.

They ended up picnicking in his office, ordering in some food and then sending Mrs. Pettibone home early.

Roxanne assumed their delayed departure was so she and Maverick could return to their elevator tryst, but as it turned out, he had an office fantasy of his own. She was just thankful the windows were tinted because he stripped her naked and held her up against the cold glass as he brought them both again to climax. She did have to admit she'd found it exhilarating, although she wondered if he had any Windex to wipe the ass mark off the glass.

Sated, she took a rain check on their planned elevator fun, and they headed back to her place. After a hot shower—which used up all the hot water—they climbed into bed and snuggled.

Maverick noticed her rubbing her bottom, which still oddly stung.

"Sorry about that."

"Sorry for what?" she asked with a frown.

Maverick explained what Psyche had done.

Roxanne sat up straight in bed. "The bitch had me shot with a love arrow? I'm going to kill her scrawny, uptight ass," she swore. "Thank Zeus the spell just reinforced what I felt for you."

"Actually, my love," Maverick said with shining eyes and a sensual smile, "you should have fallen in love with Kyle since he's the first person you saw after getting shot with it."

"Kyle? Eew. No way. I guess the arrow was a dud." Roxanne frowned and shuddered at her close call.

Maverick rolled her under him and smiled down at her. "Oh, the arrow worked fine. It just turns out your love for me was stronger than the spell."

"I guess I can't deny it anymore, can I?" she said with a wry grin. "I love you, Maverick Eros, even if you are a god and way too hot for your own good."

"And I love you more than I imagined possible, Roxanne Fortuna."

"Don't you just love a happy ending?" said a sniffling Venus, who suddenly stood at the foot of their bed.

"Oh please, they just needed a little luck with their love," said Roxanne's mother who materialized beside Venus.

Roxanne couldn't stop her laughter as her naked Cupid tried to order them out while keeping his man parts covered. They, of course, didn't listen.

She joined him in hiding under the covers, though when Ares and the Norse god arrived to see what the commotion was about.

But even under the blankets, her face red as a beet, she couldn't stop smiling.

"What's so funny?" he grumbled.

"Well, just think, I set out to screw Cupid, and with a little luck, I got exactly what I wished for."

Apparently, he liked that answer, for he kissed her then kissed her again. And again.

Epilogue

They were married on Valentine's Day at Roxanne's insistence. Maverick didn't care. He'd have given her the world if she asked. But all she wanted was him—and a chance to drive the mothers nuts.

As if her choice of cheesy dates wasn't enough to annoy both their mothers, Roxanne had gone all out with the Valentine theme and decorated his mother's ballroom in pink and red streamers. She'd also strung up Cupid cutouts—the cherub in a diaper kind with a bow and arrow. He'd especially enjoyed her laughter when he'd had to admit that the popular image of the baby—chubby-cheeked Cupid—was, in fact, how he'd looked as a youngster. She'd stopped laughing, though, when he'd rubbed her tummy and said he hoped the child she carried looked like her instead.

Now, standing in front of his friends and family, Maverick paced nervously to his father's chuckles.

"Relax, son. I'm sure you've made the right choice this time."

Maverick stopped and grinned at his father. "I know I'm making the right choice. I love her more than I ever imagined possible. I'm worried about her dress."

"Her dress? Why?" asked his father. "Didn't your mother help her have it designed and made?"

"Exactly." He couldn't help but scowl. "I swear, if she's wearing some see-through gown showing off all her assets—"

His father roared with laughter.

"It's not funny," growled Maverick. "This being in real love thing also comes with jealousy. I don't like it at all."

"You'll get used to it, even if you occasionally bash a few heads because they dared flirt with her," his father confided.

But Maverick didn't hear the fatherly admission. The music started up, a hauntingly beautiful melody that signaled the start of the ceremony. His mother came floating up the aisle first dressed in a sedate, teal-colored gown that made Maverick grin and his father's jaw drop. Venus seated herself serenely, looking every inch the mother of the groom until she winked at him mischievously.

Maverick stopped breathing as he waited. A hush fell over the crowd, and then Roxanne appeared, her arm linked with her mother's.

She looked radiant, and Maverick's heart swelled. *And to think she chose me.*

Roxanne floated down the petal-strewn aisle, her eyes locked with his and shining with love. His eyes grew suspiciously damp. *Damned dust.*

Dressed in a gown of white, overlain with lace, the heart-shaped bodice displayed her breasts to perfection—almost too much so. He'd have to cover her up for the reception.

It seemed to take forever for her to reach him, and when she placed her hand in his, Maverick could have sworn all the lovers in the world sighed with the rightness of it.

The god of love had found his one and only, and no man, god, or woman would ever tear them apart.

And as for Psyche, the one who'd tried to ruin it? He hadn't killed her. Instead, with a perverse sense of irony, he'd dragged out his trusty bow and arrow and shot her in the ass—twice— while she was stuck in an elevator with Kyle.

Nobody screws Cupid, well, no one but Roxanne, that is. Forever…

The End

Author Bio

Hello and thank you so much for reading my story.  I hope I kept you well entertained. As you might have noticed, I enjoy blending humor in to my romance. If you like my style then I have many other wicked stories that might intrigue you. Skip ahead for a sneak peek, or pay me a visit at http://www.EveLanglais.com This Canadian author and mom of three would love to hear from you so be sure to connect with me.

Facebook: http://bit.ly/faceevel
Twitter: @evelanglais
Newsletter: http://evelanglais.com/newrelease

Made in the USA
Middletown, DE
30 September 2017